Quiet Money 2

Lock Down Publications and Ca$h
Presents
Quiet Money 2
A Novel by *Trai'Quan*

Lock Down Publications

P.O. Box 944
Stockbridge, Ga 30281

Copyright 2020 by Trai'Quan
Quiet Money 2

First Edition August 2020
Printed in the United States of America

Lock Down Publications
Like our page on Facebook: Lock Down Publications @
www.facebook.com/lockdownpublications.ldp
Cover design and layout by: **Dynasty Cover Me**
Book interior design by: **Shawn Walker**
Edited by: **Shawn Walker**

Stay Connected with Us!

Text **LOCKDOWN** to 22828 to stay up-to-date with new releases, sneak peaks, contests and more…

Thank you!

Submission Guideline.

Submit the first three chapters of your completed manuscript to ldpsubmissions@gmail.com, subject line: Your book's title. The manuscript must be in a .doc file and sent as an attachment. Document should be in Times New Roman, double spaced and in size 12 font. Also, provide your synopsis and full contact information. If sending multiple submissions, they must each be in a separate email.

Have a story but no way to send it electronically? You can still submit to LDP/Ca$h Presents. Send in the first three chapters, written or typed, of your completed manuscript to:

LDP: Submissions Dept
P.O. Box 944
Stockbridge, Ga 30281

DO NOT send original manuscript. Must be a duplicate.

Provide your synopsis and a cover letter containing your full contact information.

Thanks for considering LDP and Ca$h Presents.

Trai'Quan

Prologue

Something woke him out of his slumber, he didn't know what it was. But as his senses began to come back to him, he sat up in the bed. His eyes were unfocused and his ears weren't tuned in yet. He swung his feet over the side of the b ed and inhaled deeply. Glancing around the room in its darkness, he couldn't tell if anything was wrong.

Behind him, he was aware of the shape that the call girl's body made. She was laying on her side, faced away from him. Vincent smiled when he thought about last night. He hadn't had sex that good since he was a teen. Lord knew his wife wasn't putting out these days. The old bat, all she ever did was complain about this or that, which was why he found comfort in the arms of call girls and hookers, not that it was a good thing.

Vincent sighted, he pushed himself up and made his way into the bathroom. They were in one of the more exclusive hotels on the edge of Atlantic City. One that he often used so that he could keep his relatives discreet.

Inside of the bathroom, he turned the light on and took a piss. Once he finished, he then turned and stumbled back into the room. Thinking that he might have drank too much last night. And the girl somehow managed to get him to snort a little coke with her.

When he looked up, at first, he thought that he was seeing the girl sitting on the edge of the bed. But then his old eyes, using the light from the bathroom, adjusted. And he realized that it wasn't the girl, but instead, he was looking at the form of a well-dressed man.

"How did you get in here?" Vincent stumbled as he glanced around the room.

Being on the 13th floor of the twenty-story hotel, he was puzzled as to how he got into his room, even with his balcony window open, it still baffled him due to the climb.

"Calm down, Vincent. I wouldn't want you to have a heart attack before we even had a chance to speak," the man said.

Vincent's eyes took in the leather gloves he wore. In one hand, he held a gun and what looked like a silencer on the end of it. In the other hand, he held some piece of paper.

"What do you want?" Vincent asked, as he watched him smile.

"Retribution."

"Retribution? But I don't know you," his heart began to beat faster.

"Of course, you do, Vincent. I mean, after all, you've just had my two lady friends killed. So, how could you forget me so fast?"

"You're Blacksun?"

"Yeah, something like that. But hey, how about you have a seat while we talk," Merrick stood and moved to stand in the full moon light coming through the balcony doors. It was at this time that Vincent also became aware of another form standing still right next to the curtain on the left side.

Feeling weak as realization set in on him, Vincent moved to sit upon the edge of the ed. As he did, he looked at the form of the call girl. She hadn't moved an inch.

"Oh, don't worry about her. She was dead before you awoke, but hey," Merrick hunched his shoulders.

"If you're going to kill me, then would you just get on with it? I'm already old. I don't have much else to lose in this life-time."

"Sure, you do. You see, this is more than an execution be-cause you took so much from me. You took five precious lives

7

away from me and in doing so, you've made it impossible for me to simply kill you and live my life in peace."

Vincent looked toward the door, but it wasn't a realistic option.

"Inside, deep inside, I feel pain, Vincent. This is a pain that you created and it only seems fair if I can share this pain with you. What you did was an act that gives me right to declare a vendetta against you."

"But you're not Sicilian. You're a negro. You don't live by our laws."

"That' not quite true. Through my mother's blood, I am about 30% Sicilian. In fact, her family has strong roots in Calabria, which is where the Nolrangheta exist.

"Impossible. You lie!" Vincent was outraged.

"No, but that's neither here nor there. What I'm here to offer you right now is a chance to save the lives of your wife and daughters."

He watched Vincent's eyes become large with fear.

"Did you?"

"No. I haven't killed them. But since you killed my two unborn children, it's only right if I return the favor, wouldn't you think?"

"Please. I didn't know the women were pregnant."

"It doesn't matter. What I have here is a contract. And in it, you'll sign over your 54% of your casino to me. Now, the truth of the matter is you will die tonight, but whether your family lives or not is entirely up to you."

Merrick held the contract out to him. Along with a pen. He watched as Vincent skimmed through it.

"But, Andretti wouldn't honor this. No Italian would go into business with a negro."

"You let me worry about that. Your goal is to ensure that I don't leave here and pay your family a visit. Like I've said, your life is already at its end. So, what will it be?"

Merrick watched as the Italian looked down at the paper once more. He already knew that the man would sign it and he'd write the suicide note, as well. There was no doubt about it. When he decided to visit to visit Vincent and kill him because of what he'd done, Merrick thought why should he just kill him for free? It still wouldn't erase his pain; it wouldn't bring them back.

However, he could turn his loses into opportunities. If he played his card just right, he could use this as a way for him to enter into Vincent's world. After all, he was a business man. And those Italians had a business that he would love to get in on.

ANOTHER TRAI'QUAN ORIGINAL...
Quiet Money 2

Chapter One

".... (I'm so hood).... Yeah I wear my pants below my waist and I never dance when I'm in the place, that you and yo man's is plannin to hate...."

Later, the news would read that a crooked police officer was murdered along with his entire family. Police were calling it a drug related crime, seeing as several pounds of various drugs were found. The estimated street value was around two million dollars. Police had no suspects at the time, but they are looking for any leads. Anyone with information on this case can call the hotline at the bottom of the screen...

1-800-6snitch

We'll be sure to get back to you.

***

"You might want to take a look at this."

Agent Simkins looked up as his partner, Agent Flowers, stepped up to his desk. He saw that she held some reports in her hand and reached up for them. He took a moment to look over them, at first, he wasn't sure what he was looking at. Something about an ATF investigation being trampled over. He glanced up.

"Just keep reading," she said.

He flipped the page. It seemed that the ATF were running a big sting operation involving guns and drug trafficking. Some guy, who intended to extort the informant, high jacked the shipment and destroyed the drugs.

"The next page," she pushed.

It was when he flipped the page that it really hit him. Their antagonist was some guy named Merrick, whom the ATF now suspected of extorting several other businesses throughout Georgia. Apparently, Merrick would find out that some wealthy business owners had their hand in the cookie jar and with that knowledge, he was blackmailing and extorting them. None of it could be proven, so far. None of the businesses that were suspected were talking.

"Muthafucka!" Special Agent Chester Simkins cursed.

"Wait, there's more," Agent Flowers said.

He flipped the page and read about the hit on the two girls and the kid at Zaxbeys. "Shit," he cursed.

"Seems like he's gotten himself into some deep water," Agent Flowers commented.

Agent Simkins thought about it for a minute. "Put in a call to this agent Beats. Tell him that we have an interest in this guy and ask him if he'd mind us coming up to look over the case."

"Will do."

Agent Simkins sat at his desk and thought about it. For some strange reason, his gut kept telling him that this guy Merrick was still connected to the Miami International case even if his prints did clear. Maybe he wasn't on the scene, or he hadn't touched anything himself. There was 88 million US dollars missing and there was no way to tell where this kid got his money. So, until he got some answers, he was interested in this guy, Merrick Blacksun.

* * *

Ameed was actually too hard to cry about it. The break up came on top of everything else. With the hit on Kenya and Tammy and then him telling her that he had another woman pregnant, he really wasn't mad that one day Pat packed her things and decided to move back to Augusta. She said Atlanta just had too much going on for her. So, he'd broken bread with her, she didn't come to Atlanta broke, so he wasn't about to let her leave messed up. Besides, he understood what she was going through.

Ameed learned the 48 laws of power in his 12th grade year of school. He made it a habit to *Never Outshine the Master.* Merrick had placed him over the M&A Corporation, or at least everything that went on in Atlanta. He didn't have time to cry about losing Patrice.

"I reach into your soul like ether, teach you the king, you know you, God son across the belly, I prove you've lost already."

He snatched the phone up off the dash board of the new Escalade SRX he'd recently purchased. It was a nice, deep, burgundy and had Giovanni 20-inch rims on it.

"Peace. What's the deal?"

"I thought we were having lunch together."

Damn, he thought as he turned off Candler Rd onto Mcaffe Rd. He drove up and made a right on Columbia, then the next turn onto Snapfinger Rd.

"Yeah, yeah. We gone hook up Di. But I need to check in wit' my BM right quick. Were you at?"

"I'll meet you at Miss Ann's at 1:30."

The call ended. He pulled up into the sub division and then into the driveway of a nice house. There was a black LS coupe in the driveway. He parked and then stepped out. Ameed walked up to the house and pressed the doorbell, then waited. When the door opened, Ameed found himself standing there facing the pregnant woman.

Originally, Princess was 5'7" and 132 pounds. She had a nice figure and the most exotic look. She looked like a Korean mixed with Brazilian or something.

"It sure took you long enough." She turned and walked back into the house.

"Yeah, well, I had some things to look into." Ameed closed the door then followed her into the den area where she sat in front of her computer and continued what she'd been doing.

"Does anyone know when Merrick will be back?" she asked.

"Not really," he replied.

Merrick had been in New Jersey since the end of December last year and it was the third of February now. He didn't exactly know what Merrick was up to but he knew that Bradly, the crooked police, was dead along with the rest of his family. And whatever Merrick had going on, he had Monk with him.

"Well, here's your next target." Princess turned the computer screen so that he could see it.

"AutoZone?" he asked with some reserve.

Princess picked up on it and sighed. "Look, this guy has a lot going on. He's buying, or rather trading, stolen parts with another guy in Mobile, Alabama. It's more of a chop shop for expensive cars. I'd say they bring in something like $800 thousand a month," she explained.

Ameed whistled. That was a pretty big operation. That was about three million a year on just that hustle alone. "And these fools actually tell women their business like that?" He was still confused about that part.

"We learn a lot from pillow talk. Most of you men can't wait to brag about what you have or the illegal shit you do. Especially to a woman who isn't your wife," she explained.

Her words reminded him of the third rule of power, which was, *Conceal Your Intentions*. That was what these wealthy guys who couldn't get pleasure at home didn't do. They were so quick to brag, trying to impress these high-class call girls, thinking that they would become her favorite, that they revealed their deepest, darkest secrets to them. That, he knew, was stupid.

＊ ＊ ＊

"I can't believe you gave that guy your number," Monica said.

The three of them exited the South Dekalb Mall carrying their shopping bags and walked across the parking lot, about to leave.

"I mean, why wouldn't I give it to him? He's cute," Jen said.

"Maybe it's because he goes to Columbia," Crystal put in.

They were talking about a guy that Jen met as they were leaving one of the stores they'd shopped at.

"So, we're not allowed to date guys at Columbia?" Jen asked. But she knew what they meant. To them, Columbia High School was a little too hood. There seemed to be a whole lot of violence at Columbia and something new was happening damn near every day.

"I'm just saying. If that's what you're looking for," Monica said. "Then that's on you."

They reached the 2010, Midnight purple, Denali that was sitting on the 20-inch Pinnacle, chrome saw blade, rims. The truck itself was a birthday gift that Jen received from Merrick for her 17th birthday. She pulled her key chain out and pressed the car alarm button and the doors unlocked.

All three of them were 17 and in their last year of school. Jen stood 5'9" and had brown skin with brown and green eyes. She kept all of her 125 pounds packed into measurements of 34B-32-36, with the work out habit she developed with her brother. Her friends weren't as healthy in some regards. Monica was 5'5 and healthy, but had an exotic look, while Crystal was 5'7 and a little bigger than Jen.

"So, what do you think your brothers would say if they knew you were talking to a thug?" Crystal asked.

They'd all gotten into the truck and Jen started it then began to exit the parking lot. Everyone they knew in Atlanta thought Ameed was her brother, too.

"They do not get in my business," Jen said. She noticed that she needed gas so she looked around for a gas station and ended up pulling into an Ameco.

"Which on of y'all gone fill up while I go pay?" Jen asked.

"I'll do it," Crystal told her.

Exiting the truck, Jen started towards the store but was looking through her Gucci bag so she wasn't really paying much attention. She didn't see the black Ford Excursion pull up from the opposite direction. Entering the store, Jen went to the freezers and grabbed three sodas then walked up to stand in the line. While standing there, she looked up as a group of guys entered the store. She could tell that they were all older than her, maybe even older than Snipes. But she could also see that they were gang bangers by the six-point Star of David on one of their T-Shirts.

"Hold up. Damn, Shawty. What's up?" a dark skinned one asked as he stopped next to her.

Jen knew she looked good in her Seven Jeans, three-inch Jimmy Choo platforms, Coogi sweater and the Ladies presidential Rolex that Ameed gave her for her birthday. She didn't feel like she was obligated to respond to these gang bangers, slash dope boys and that's what they looked like.

"Oh. You must be too good to speak," he continued.

"Damn, you must be losing yo touch, Shawty," one of the other ones said.

Now the other people in the store were noticing, especially when the first guy stepped in front of her.

"Uh, excuse you," Jen said.

"Oh. So, you can talk." The guy smiled down at her. He was 6'1, dark skinned and about 188 pounds. He was dressed like he stood on the corner all day and sold drugs. "Look, my names Sosa and I just want to get to know you."

"Nah, I'm good. Could you please move out of my way?" she stepped around him.

Sosa couldn't help himself. He cocked his head to watch her ass in those jeans. "Okay, hold up. You just gone bypass this shit, Shawty. What? Those contacts you wearing ain't clear enough?"

At this point, his boys had walked out of the store so he was hoping his game would get through. The lil bitch was just too fine, but he could tell that she was one of them stuck up girls, too.

"Listen," Jen looked him up and down. "I don't know who you think you are, but I can assure you, I'm not interested. Besides, you fall into my *don't do* category, anyway."

"Your *don't do*? Shawty, what ya trying to say?"

"I don't do drugs, drug dealers, gangs, or gang bangers and I definitely don't do flexin' ass niggaz. Is that clear enough for you?" The person in front of her moved and she found herself at the counter. Jen placed the sodas on it and passed the cashier her Visa card.

"Sounds like you hatin' to me, Shawty. You need to get that shit out yo system," Sosa stated.

The lady behind the register ran her card and Jen told her to add the gas. She handed the card back and put the sodas into a bag. Jen grabbed the bag and her card then turned and walked out the door.

She was almost to the truck when Sosa, who followed behind her, grabbed her elbow. "Whoa, whoa, whoa, Shawty. I was still talking to you."

But as soon as she stopped, Jen's eyes locked in on his hand. The one touching her.

"Hey, boy! Get yo hands off my girl!" Monica called out as she opened the door and got out.

"My bad, Shawty." Sosa released her and held his hand up to the sky.

"How old are you?" Jen asked.

He smiled. "Twenty-two, Shawty, I'm about to be twenty-three and I'm a made nigga. My check got major zeros on it," he bragged.

"Uh huh, but I'm sixteen, which means yo ass will go to prison if my brothers don't see about you first. So, if yo business is that good then why don't you focus on it and leave jail bait alone?"

"Come on, baby. You've got to be older. Shit, when is yo birthday?"

But Jen just shook her head then stepped around him and went to join her friends.

Sosa watched as the young bitch got into the Denali she was driving. He definitely didn't think that she was sixteen, but just in case, he memorized her tag number. His older sister worked at the Dekalb County jail and he was gone ask her to look it up for him. He just wasn't about to accept that the bitch wasn't feeling him. Not him, the young Sosa, the nigga who had the whole Eastwick apartments on smash. If anything, the bitch was pushing another nigga'z whip and didn't want neither one of the other hoes she was with to tell on her. Yeah, that's what it was he thought. So, he decided to give her another shot.

"And if you feel me, put yo hands up (Hood) my hood niggaz gone and stand up..."

Chapter Two

Merrick stepped out of the house and pulled the trench coat tighter as the wind whipped around him. The house was a nice house in the Linden section of Union County, which was Northeastern New Jersey, over on Auther Kill and at the mouth of the Rahway River. It wasn't far from Elizabeth.

Out in the streets, parked next to the curb and right in front of the house, was the brand-new black on black, 2010 Lincoln Navigator. He watched as Monk stood with his back against the truck, smoking a cigarette, then Merrick walked down the steps and onto the side walk.

"We gotta ride out to Brooklyn," he said as he walked around to the passenger side. "The old lady said the person who can help me is out in Bensonhurst. Come on."

They both got into the Navigator with Monk driving. As he started the truck and put it into drive, Merrick's mind went into overtime. He'd taken the contract to another lawyer and a judge in Atlantic City. They'd both said that the contract was good, especially since they'd had Vincent write the suicide note. In it he'd mentioned that he had been in so much debt that he eventually had to sell his shares in the casino. There was a small mention of it being sold to a black guy who was supposed to be Italian. The news painted the picture of a horribly shameful scene. So, Vincent had killed the hooker he'd been with and jumped, that was the extent of what had really happen. Or so the news said.

Merrick hadn't taken the contract to the other shareholder yet. He went to the lawyer first, but it was the judge who explained the complications to him. While the contract itself was legally binding, especially with Vincent acknowledging in his suicide letter that he did sell it to a black guy, the problem would be that the Italian's wouldn't want to do business with someone who had no ties to their life style. The issues would revolve around trust, loyalty and Omerta. Most Italians felt that blacks had very little real understanding of the three. Merrick explained to the judge that he did have an Italian kinship, and after a moment's thought, the judge explained to him that *if* he could prove some kind of blood ties with a real legitimate Italian family, then that would give him some grounds. It would be even better if the Italian family would be willing to stand up for him because the issue would be taken before the commission.

The commission was the board of bosses. It included five bosses in New York, two bosses in New Jersey, two bosses in the Detroit/Chicago area, a boss in Arizona, three bosses in Nevada, and three bosses in California. However, this did not mean that these were the Dons of these cities. A Boss was one who controlled and oversaw the business and financial aspects of the families. While a Boss had nearly the same power as a Don, a Don could overrule the commission simply because he wanted to. The only way the commission could overturn a Don's decision would be to take it to the family board of Don's and Capo's, which was in Italy.

Merrick thought about all of that as he left his great grandmother's house. He hadn't seen her since he was eight but she remembered his eyes. She even asked after his sister and his mother. When he explained to her that there was a need for him to have a sponsor, he thought she wouldn't help.

"Our family name may not carry a lot of weight," the old woman had said. "We were called Cattani back then, it was our true last name. We were poor farmers in the old country. Some say that ours was a tampered blood line since the days of Hannibal." She laughed and coughed a little.

Merrick sat there respectfully and watched the fragile old lady sitting across from him.

"We made our mark when Francis Cattani the second, set out to grow grapes and ended up growing the exotic white grapes, which eventually earned him a contract with some of the older families." She paused with a faraway look on her face, deep in memories. "Francis Cattani, the third actually married into the Gambino hierarchy. He took his wife from amongst a family that was second or third cousins to the Gambino's. So, when his family moved here to the states, our family, we Corsicans, still had the blood of Hannibal within us. Thus, our babies sometimes came out with darker skin than those from Sicily Island."

Here she paused and he asked if he could get her anything. Merrick went into the kitchen and brought her a glass of water. He retook his seat and waited while she sipped the water.

She looked up into his face as she spoke, "Our family wasn't the only one with dark blood," she continued. "You see, as long as it was a marriage of Italian and Sicilian, the darkness didn't get any darker. Somehow when we branched out and moved to New Jersey, your grandfather met your grandmother, who wasn't exactly black. She was Latino, which is why your mother doesn't show the traits of her Italian bloodline. Your Grandfather, my son, was guided by his heart."

Silence came between them as they both sunk deep in thought. Merrick had never met his grandfather so he didn't know what kind of man he was.

"Francis Cattani IV. That's who you need to help you," she picked up again. "He's our cousin and he's always been in good standing with the families." She dropped her voice to a whisper, "I think he may be a mad man himself, I'm not sure."

He watched her smile then she reached into a pocket in her dress and withdrew a ring. It was a large ring so he knew that it was a men's ring. She held it up and showed him that it was silver and the top of it consisted of a white rose.

"It belonged to my husband," she said in a normal voice. "I know he was a made-man, but he wasn't high up the ladder. They only called on him to do certain jobs for them. He never said no when they called and most of the times it would be Francis who called." The old woman leaned forward. She reached out and took Merrick's left hand. She gently pushed the ring onto his ring finger and said, "When you meet Francis and tell him who you are, tell him that I placed this on your finger myself." She smiled and watched as he looked at the ring. It was unique with in its self. "I don't' know how much life I have left in me," she told him and he noticed that she was crying. "But I feel that I've been blessed to see you again and hope that I will be able to see your sister again before I get to my final resting place. Know this though, as long as I still breathe, you have a home here."

Merrick looked down at the ring that seem to fit his finger as if it had been made for him. One would almost say that he'd had the ring designed himself. He saw, out of the corner of his eye, that Monk looked over at it, too. "My great grandmother gave me this," he said.

It wasn't that Monk couldn't talk, but more like he didn't waste words. He spoke only when it was necessary. Merrick noticed that they were in Brooklyn and headed towards the Bensonhurst section so he gave Monk the address that his great grandmother had given him. He had also made up his mind that he would make sure his mother and Jen came to visit her once he had this business situated.

The address led them to a pastry store, which sat in the heart of Bensonhurst. Not a very large building, in fact it would be considered small. Monk found a parking space and they both exited the SUV. Merrick was wearing a nice two-piece Armani suit with Vasquez dress shoes, while Monk wore Gurtex boots,

Parasuco jeans, a black T-shirt and a Brooks Brothers Trench coat.

When Merrick pulled the door open and they stepped inside, there was only one customer at the counter talking to the older Italian behind it. The guy behind the counter was of an average height, but looked solidly built. In fact, if he had been taller, he would have been compared to a brick mason.

Upon entering the store, Monk took up a position near the front while Merrick walked over to one end of the counter and started looking down into the display case. There were all types of pastries on display.

"Alright, alright, you can have the red velvet. I'll do it up just as you say. When will you be back from your trip?" the Italian asked.

"Next Thursday," the woman replied.

"It'll be done. Now if you will, I have other customers who need to see me," he said.

The woman glanced behind her and saw the young, well-dressed, black man pretending to look at pastries. Being from Bensonhurst, she knew how things really were so she excused herself and exited the store.

"What can I do for you, gentlemen?" Francis Cattani IV asked.

Merrick glanced up. "Is that a Pecan Pie with lemon crust?"

"Sure, it is," Francis smiled. "My own recipe. Best pie you'll find in Brooklyn."

"I'd like one. I think great grandmother would really like it," Merrick stated.

Merrick turned and faced the older man. He watched as the man looked at him closely and then looked at Monk. "I'm looking for Francis Cattani."

"And you would be?"

Merrick moved closer to where Francis stood. "My great grandmother told me to show you this." He held his hand out with the ring on it and watched as Francis gazed at the beauty of the ring.

"And did Agatha tell you how your great grandfather, my great cousin, came across the ring?"

"She told me what she suspected, but she only told me what I needed to know. I need your help," he told him then he watched as Francis looked to Monk once more.

"Have your guy lock the door and turn over the closed sign. Then follow me to the back, we can talk back there."

They proceeded to the back, where Merrick explained about himself and what he was doing. Then Francis outlined the rules and the structure of the commission. In the end he agreed to sponsor him because he knew the history of their blood line.

Chapter Three

"I'm so tied up on my own, I'm so tired of being alone. Won't you help me girl, just as soon as you can...."
–Al Green

"Ayo, Shawty, hold up. That's that bitch right there."

Sosa was about to pass by the Subway on Memorial Drive that was across the street from the CVS, when Tino saw the Denali parked in the subway parking lot.

After looking back, Sosa made the necessary turns that took them back to the Subway. They pulled into the parking lot and parked right next to the Denali. Sosa knew that the lil bitch had lied to him. His sister found out the bitch's name was Jennifer Blacksun and she was seventeen. The SUV was in her name.

They got out, Sosa, Tino and his partner, Head. All three entered the Subway and as soon as he stepped in, Sosa's eyes landed on the lil thot. She was looking too good in her Farrago jeans, Prada wedges, and a Northface shirt. She was even wearing a few jewels that went with it. But she wasn't alone, she was sitting at a table with the little, pudgy girl she was with that day and two young ass niggaz who looked like they went to a prep school or something.

Feeling himself, Sosa didn't see any logical reason to respect the two lames.

"Shawty! Damn, Shawty, you ain't have to lie to a nigga," he said as he came to a stop next to their table.

Jen looked up and rolled her eyes. She didn't know why this nigga was stalking her.

"Jen, you know this guy?" The boy she was sitting next to asked as he realized Sosa was talking to her and not Monica.

"No, I do not know him," she told Tony. She looked up at Sosa. "Could you please just leave me alone?" she asked nicely.

Sosa looked down at the table then he looked at everyone sitting there. "I guess this is yo lil boyfriend, huh? But listen, Shawty, nigga' ain't getting no check sitting around in Subway, and a nigga like me, I've got a big check, Shawty. Look at these rocks." He showed her the rings on both hands and his iced-out watch. He did have a lot of ice on.

"Ahem," Tony, her date spoke up. "Look, bruh. It seems obvious that she ain't into you. So why don't you just let us have this little bit?"

"What?" Sosa laughed. "Shawty, this nigga must be gay. Let him have this lil bit. Nigga, do you know who I am?"

"Nah, I don't, and I'm not gay either."

This caused Sosa to smile. "Oh, yeah. Shawty, you wanna go outside and fight for ole girl? I bet you punk out, Shawty," Sosa antagonized.

Jen watched as Tony looked across the table at his partner, Freddy. They were both 18 and neither one was a thug, but when he looked at her, Jen realized that he was going to try to impress her.

"A'ight, let's go," Tony said.

"What?" Jen jumped in. "No. Tony you don't have to fight this clown. You came here with me so I'm leaving here with you," she explained.

"Nah, Shawty," Sosa said. "This nigga loose, it's me and you. Fuck that."

As Tony pushed up out of the seat, she looked at Sosa and his two henchmen. There was no way that Tony was going to win this fight, so as they started towards the door, she pulled out her phone and called Ameed.

* * *

"My nigga, Jack of Spades, what's up, Shawty?"

At the sound of his nickname, Judah looked behind him. At the moment he and Ameed stood at the freezer in the store, about to grab the two Hennessy Blacks. He had to get them because Ameed wasn't 21 yet and he had just turned 21 a few weeks ago. When he looked back, he saw this nigga, Cutt, standing in the aisle behind them. Closing the door with the two drinks in his hand, Judah turned to face his ex-partner.

"What's up, Cutt?" he asked, not liking the evil, shifty looking smile Cutt had on his face.

Cutt, AKA Cut Throat, had at one time been Judah's right hand, back when they were in the dope game. But things changed, prison changed Judah, especially the two years he did at Hays State Prison. The shit was like a war zone with the gangs.

At Hays, life wasn't what most people's families were thinking. Niggaz were either fighting or stabbing each other on a regular, or getting raped by the booty bandits. If a nigga was too soft and couldn't defend himself, he joined a gang. The gangs were basically the new prison protection plan. At one point, niggaz became Muslim because they were soft, now they joined gangs.

Hays was an experience that Judah wasn't willing to go through again. So, when he came home and met Ameed through his older sister Princess, he jumped on the team and started making legal money.

"Damn, Shawty. You lookin' at a nigga like I owe you money or something," Cutt stated.

Judah almost said, *"or something"*, but he kept his mouth shut.

Ameed had pulled off, he didn't like to associate with hood niggaz that caused unnecessary problems.

"Just gone and say what's on yo mind, bruh," Judah said.

"Nuthin', Shawty, but damn, can't a nigga just stop and say what's up?"

Judah started towards the front of the store, with Cutt following him. There was a reason Judah didn't want to deal with Cutt, because Cutt was a hater, the shit was just in his blood. He was one of those niggaz who could be wearing the same pair of Nike's that you wore, but still hate on you because of the way you rocked yours.

"Shit, nigga. You mean you actually took time out of running Coventon walk. Just to come say what's up to me? Damn." Judah paused to glance around. "I must be doing something you just now heard about."

"Now see, Shawty that was just cold. It ain't even like that," Cutt said while giving Judah a look like he was hurt.

But Judah knew better. "Shawty, a nigga wasn't even looking for you. I just stopped to get some gas, but hey, if it's gone be like that. I'll keep it moving Shawty," Cutt said. "Oh, and tell Princess I said what's up."

With that said, Judah watched him exit the store. But he wasn't stupid, he didn't believe the excuse. Nine times out of ten Cutt heard that he was working at M&A limo services or even saw his own smoke grey, 2010 Escalade EXT parked at the gas pump. Either somebody told him about Judah's new job and ride, or he'd seen it.

"Yo, what's up?" Judah asked. He'd paid for the drinks and stepped outside where Ameed stood next to the truck, on his phone.

"We need to get to the Subway on Memorial, ASAP," Ameed stated and they both hopped in the truck.

* * *

Cutt was sitting inside of his Dodge Durango, parked up the street at one of the traps. He could still see the gas station from where he sat. He watched as Judah came out and joined the other nigga at the truck.

"Nigga, think his shit don't stink," he thought to himself. *"Got a new ride, now he better than everybody else."*

Cutt was a presendential nigga and a manipulator. He'd long ago saw that Judah had a skill when it came to hustling. His flip game was nice. So, Cutt made it a point to befriend him and pretend to be friends. To him, it was all about the paper, but in truth, Cutt really didn't know why he didn't like Judah, but he did know that he'd *never* liked him. Even when they were hustling together, before he caught that little bid. Sometimes he would be sitting there smiling at the nigga while silently and inside of his head, be wondering what Judah would do if he just up and punched him in the jaw. For no reason other than to do the shit.

He was wondering what this nigga really had going on. That job driving limos couldn't be paying that much, which meant the nigga had something else going on and Cutt wanted to know what. It had been a long time since he'd robbed a stupid nigga.

* * *

When the Escalade pulled up there was a crowd standing around in a circle. When Ameed stepped out, Judah was right behind him as he pushed his way through the people. Inside the circle, Jen was standing in front of another young nigga whose lip was bleeding and it looked like his eye was about to swell. Ameed saw another nigga standing across from them and two other's standing behind him.

"See, it's like I told you," Sosa was saying. "Shawty, you need to let this loser go and start winning."

"Lame ass nigga, you better be glad my brothers ain't here," Jen called out. "Then everybody would see how tough you really are."

"Bitch, please. Ain't nobody fuckin' wit' Sosa and you can take that to the bank, Shawty."

It was at this point that Ameed made his presence known. He stepped into the circle and right between Jen and the nigga, Sosa. "What's up? You alright?"

Jen smiled. Then looked around Ameed. "Now we gone see how bad yo ass is. Meet my brother, Ameed. Punk!" she spat.

Ameed turned to look at the nigga. This nigga was lighter than him by some and slightly shorter, but he looked like he could fight. "Before I disrespect you in front of yo peoples, how old are you?"

"Disrespect me?" Sosa became extra cocky. "Nigga, you ain't even built like that, Shawty." He looked Ameed up and down. "Lookin' like you work a 9 to 5, but on the strength, Shawty, I'm 22. Why?"

"Two reasons, first, I didn't want to be beating on a kid, which it looks like you just did." He nodded towards Tony. "Second, nigga, you too old to be pushing up on my baby sister anyway and you called her the B-word, too."

Sosa laughed. "Oh, Shawty, you mad cause I called the lil freak a bitch?"

"Yeah, that's the word."

Ameed didn't even think to remove his good clothes. Instead, assuming this nigga was a tough guy, Ameed lunged forward and threw a three piece that caught Sosa off guard. A left jab, right jab, left hook. Two connected, but as he stepped in real close and started dropping body shots on him, Sosa was thrown off by the speed with which the nigga moved. He couldn't even throw up a defense let alone return the favor.

Ameed shot a left, right hook into his kidney and came up with an upper cut. It clipped Sosa's jaw slightly, yet enough to knock him back into the arms of his boys, who held him back when he acted like he wanted to continue to fight.

"Yeah, at least somebody got some common sense," Ameed said. "And on the real, nigga, stay away from my li'l sister. You should be out there chasing grown women, not high school kids."

"Nigga, this ain't over." Sosa raised his voice. "We gone meet again and the next time, I will bust that ass, Shawty. Believe that!"

Ameed didn't bite the bait. He turned and saw that Jen and her friends were alright, then waited until they got into the truck before he walked back to Judah's ride.

He was thinking about giving Jen a lady's .380.

* * *

"Listen, Duke," Judah said as he whipped the Escalade in and out of traffic. "I know that nigga, Sosa. He's a flashy dope boy and he Gangster Disciple."

"And?" Ameed asked.

Since moving to Atlanta, Ameed hadn't actually been as wild as he had been in Augusta. Another thing he learned in the 48 Laws was to *Re-create Yourself.* Most of the time, people believed in the illusion you gave them.

"You might have a problem with the nigga, he's stupid. But that's because of his uncle," Judah explained to him. "His uncle is the brick man. He hangs out with a lot of the rappers. Nigga owns Club Fire. His name is Baby Kirk. They been calling him that for years because he grew up in Kirkwood." Judah ran it down to him.

Ameed heard what Judah said and at the same time he kept thinking about what Merrick had told him. That he would be responsible for keeping the business in order, while he was up state. Merrick also told him not to do anything that he wouldn't do. Ameed realized that for Merrick to give him that much control, he had to trust that Ameed would do what was right for the business. Getting pulled into a street conflict wasn't right for business.

One of the things he admired about Merrick was the way that he used his mind. Merrick would see the problem, separate himself from it and then analyze it from every angle. He would consider all of the possible issues that could come with each situation and there would be a plan for that which couldn't be avoided.

Ameed was doing that now, making plans. In case this, so-called street thug, became more disrespectful.

Chapter Four

"Its 7:00 on the dot, I'm in my drop top, cruisin' the streets, I've got a real pretty-pretty little thing that's waiting for me."
–Usher Nice & Slow

The Twilight Casino and Hotel wasn't the biggest or most lavish establishment in Atlantic City, there were many more. This Casino and Hotel consisted of five stories. The first floor consisted of the registration area and the restaurant, while the 60,000 square feet of the second floor housed the casino. The third and fourth floors were suite's that ran $1,500.00 a night, but on the 5th floor were Presidential suites and they ran every bit of $3,000.00.

The thing that Merrick noticed was that the Casino was in a bad way. How it made money he didn't know, especially when what was before him looked like a bootleg version of a Casino. Before he and Monk even walked in, the first thing he noticed was that the outside of the building looked old. Inside the desk looked even older, as if the place hadn't been remodeled since the 70's or 80's. Even the restaurant, which only seemed to have about ten people dining in it, looked like a vision from 'Back to the Future'. When they reached the casino, it was even more of a disappointment. There were a few people inside but no more than 50, whereas it could hold as many as 2,000 people.

Merrick walked through slowly, he guessed that the few people inside assumed he was another customer, but he was taking in the nightmare, along with another headache. When the idea to take over the casino came into his head, he thought that he would be getting his feet into a bigger piece of the world. He didn't know anything about stocks or the stock market, so he couldn't take the chance of trying to invest his money and end up losing. What he did know a little about was gambling.

Merrick somehow found himself at a blackjack table, watching as the woman dealing the cards made it look very professional. If it wasn't for her worn and old uniform, she might've been able to keep the two guys at the table's attention.

"Excuse me."

Merrick looked behind him and saw a nerdy looking white guy weaning a cheap suit. "You're talking to me?"

"Yes, sir." The guy nodded. "You are Mr. Blacksun, right? Mr. Merrick Blacksun?"

"That would be me."

"Great." The guy smiled. "Mr. Luiz asked me to come get you. I'm to bring you up to the office."

Merrick watched as he nodded towards what looked like a VIP skylight box, but the windows were all mirrored glass, which meant that someone could stand inside and watch the whole Casino. He also knew that Andretti Luiz had received a call from the Atlantic City Boss as well as the New Jersey Boss, which was why he'd been expected. So, Merrick turned and followed the mousy looking white guy who led them to a set of stairs.

The 53-year-old Andretti Luiz was not what Merrick had expected. When the door was opened, it was done by one of the two body guards who stood outside of it. Merrick stepped in behind the Mouse and Monk was behind him. There was a large desk inside the office and standing behind the desk was a short, fat, Italian man that reminded him of Danny DeVito when he played in the movie Casino, but he wasn't quite that short. He was 5'7' and had to be over two-hundred pounds. The guy wore what didn't necessarily look like a cheap suit, but it was old. Merrick watched as he forced a smile.

"So, you're the guy that made Vincent kill himself?"

Merrick also noticed that this guy wore a lot of jewelry. It kind of looked like costume jewelry though. "I hate to break it to you, but I didn't *make* Vincent do anything," Merrick told him.

"Yeah, yeah, a'ight," Andretti said. "So, I gets this call to come out to the big house in Liz and they tell me that I've got to do business wit' ya. But I tell them that I don't want to do business wit' ya, so the fuckin boss puts me in a chicken wing, wit' my arm up behind my back...." He pauses in his story then continues. "So, I say okay. Maybe I cans do business wit' ya. So, what do you know about running a Casino?" He asked.

The thing was, Merrick now owned 54% of the whole casino, which actually put him in control. He was the one who would make the decisions and his first decision was made when he met with the Atlantic City Boss. Merrick made a deal to give him more of the taxes coming from the Casino, but, he had to first get the establishment in order.

"Very little," Merrick said. "I understand the basic concept and the goal being to make money. However, from what I saw coming in, this place is losing money."

"No shit, wise guy," Andretti said as he moved from behind the desk and went to stand where he could look out the window.

"We're barely staying afloat," he stated. "The only money we're making is just enough to keep the commission from shutting us down. I had plans to buy Vinnies share and make a deal with the Boss. One where I'd give him a percentage and a bigger tax while he financed me to remodel the place. But," he hunched his shoulders.

Merrick walked over. The mousy white guy was still standing next to the desk while Monk stood by the door. He looked out into the casino. "How much would it take?"

"To do the casino? Pissh." Andretti looked back to the nerdy white guy. "Berry's the accountant, he keeps the books. You'll have to ask him."

Merrick turned and looked at Berry. "Berry, how much to renovate the entire building?" He watched as Berry's eyes grew.

"We ain't got nowhere near that kind of money," Andretti replied. "That's how Vinnie went into debt in the first place, trying to get money."

Merrick ignored him and continued looking to Berry, who wasn't sure what to do. "Well?"

"You're serious?" Berry questioned. "Just a moment." He moved behind the desk and started tapping the keys on the computer. It took a moment. "Uh, to completely restore the building, it would take about 5 million, give or take."

Merrick thought about it. "Okay, what about a complete upgrade? What if we wanted to make everything exclusive? Like these other casinos up and down the strip," he asked.

Berry typed a few more keys. Then looked up. "Between 10 to 12 million," he stated.

Merrick thought it over. The money wasn't the issue, he could put the 12 million into it with no problem and add his 54% to the M&A corporation. "And how long would it take?" He asked.

"We'd have to close the hotel and casino in order to do it right. It'll take three to four months," Berry estimated.

Merrick turned to Andretti. "I'm willing to foot the bill under one condition," he said.

"Ah, what?"

"Instead of calling it the Twilight, we change the name to Cattani's."

* * *

"I don't know how this part is going to turn out," Merrick said as he sat next to Monk on the plane. "But it shouldn't be all that hard. We just deliver Sirrelli's message and hopefully nothing crazy will happen," he said.

Monk turned his head and looked at him in a funny way. "Yeah. We might have to get some guns."

* * *

Louis *Lou* Sirrelli was the commission appointed Boss over the Atlantic City gaming society. Which meant that he controlled everything in Atlantic City and collected the taxes from all of the businesses. At seventy-one years old, Lou earned his position the hard way and he learned through life that nothing was worth having ever came easy.

This was why he'd sent Merrick to Texas. A few years ago, they'd acquired interest in an oil company. The good favor came when a big gambler allowed himself to fall so deep into debt that the only way he could get out of it was by signing over some stock in his oil company. So, now Lou owned 20% in the company itself. The only problem was, this guy started playing dodge ball lately and Lou couldn't get a straight answer out of him.

When Francis Canatti called and explained the situation with a distant cousin of his being the one who Vincent sold his share of the Casino to, Lou stepped in as a favor to Francis. However, just as he'd told Francis, this cousin would also have to do him a favor.

* * *

His plane landed in Texas and with Monk beside him, Merrick stepped off the private charter jet and they walked to the terminal. Getting through it didn't take long and soon they were renting an Airport rental car. Monk punched the address into the GPS and they pulled away from the airport. The drive was long to some extent, but it wasn't boring because he'd never been to Texas before, so the sights were worth something.

They soon pulled into the parking lot of a very large building that looked like it was made of glass. There was a large sign at the entrance that read *Cobar Gas & Oil Company.* Monk eventually found a parking space and together they headed for the door.

Once inside, Merrick walked up to the front desk. "Excuse me Miss," he said to the lady behind the desk. "My name is Merrick Blacksun and I have an appointment with Mr. Jefferson."

Merrick was self-conscious of the way the middle-aged white woman sized him up. He thought that it must have been the Tricots St. Raphael suit.

"One moment, Mr. Blacksun," she finally stated after her visual inspection. She reached over, lifted the phone and spoke into it, "The appointment is here. Sirrelli said he had his people make it, he said there wouldn't be any conflict." The woman's conversation lasted just at two minutes. She hung up the phone and spoke to Merrick. "Take those elevators over there and go up to the 39th floor. When you get off the elevator, there will be a desk to your left. Give the secretary your name and she'll help you," she directed.

"Thank you," Merrick said, then turned and started towards the elevators.

The woman at the desk on the 39th floor took him directly to the office behind her and opened the door. Merrick walked into a spacious office with a large window behind an oak desk.

"Mr. Blacksun, it's nice to meet you. Please have a seat."

The young guy at the desk in front of him indicated the seat across from him. Merrick was mentally trying to figure out the sense in all of this. He'd expected to be meeting some older tycoon who owned and ran an oil company. This guy couldn't have been more than 30, but he wore his suit with confidence and was well shaved.

"Now tell me what is it that I can do for you?"

"Look, you are aware of the fact that this visit is on behalf of Louis Sirrelli, right?" He watched as the guy nodded. "Then you know that Mr. Sirrelli sees your avoiding him as a business conflict."

"Well, yes, I can see how things would look that way. Mr. Sirrelli has to understand that this type of business isn't like the business he's used to," Mr. Jefferson explained.

Merrick wasn't sure if he understood what this guy was saying, business was business. Especially when you'd just gambled away 20% of a company. "I'm afraid I don't understand. "Mr. Sirrelli gave me the impression that you signed over some stock to him, due to a credit marker you had."

"True, I mean that was the way that it appeared," Mr. Jefferson stated. "Unfortunately, I don't own the company. My grandfather does and he's still, somehow, hanging on to his last breath. Upon the old man's death, I do inherit the company and I will honor my agreement with Mr. Sirrelli. However, that doesn't seem to be anytime soon. When I made that deal the old man was in bad health, but since then his health has improved some." Mr. Jefferson hunched his shoulders. "How was I to know?"

Merrick sat there and processed the information. He pulled out his latest cellphone and looked up. "Mind if I make a call?"

"No, go ahead."

He stood and walked to the far end of the office where he called Sirrelli. Merrick took a few minutes to explain the situation to him then he listened.

"Alright," Sirrelli sighed. "If there's nothing else that can be done, you and your guy can return. I'll see you when you get back."

Merrick ended the call, however, he still had thoughts running through his head. He was trying to figure out how he would handle the situation if the guy owed him money. "Thank you for your time, Mr. Jefferson," he said as Monk rose and they both left.

* * *

The elder Mr. Jefferson paused part of the way up the stairs to deal with his uncontrollable cough. It was so bad that he had to bend over and use one hand to brace against the wall, but it only lasted for a few seconds. When it was over, he continued on his way up to his bedroom. Everyone else who lived in the Ranch house was asleep, all 22 of its staff and what little of his family he still held close to him. There weren't many and most of those were his great grandkids. His own children were all dead, except for one, a daughter that somehow ended up on drugs. It was a wonder to him that she'd out lived the others.

He finally made it to his bedroom where he sat on the edge of the bed for a moment. At the time, he could barely keep his eyes open so he knew that sleep would come easily. He leaned back and swung his feet up onto the bed. As his head hit the pillow, his eye's drifted shut and his breathing became easy.

He was comfortable and peaceful. So much so that he didn't notice the shadow as it detached itself from the wall and stepped over to the bed, looking down at the elderly man. The shadow reached over and lifted the extra pillow from the bed then placed it over the older man's face and pressed down.

The old man's instincts were what caused him to try and fight against the hands holding the pillow to his face. But the struggle didn't last long, in fact, it lasted less than two minutes. When the old man's body stop moving, the shadow replaced the pillow and smoothed the pillow case. Then, just as it had come, the shadow faded into the darkness, becoming one with the night.

Trai'Quan

Chapter Five

"I embrace you like napalm, blowed up- left chest face gone. How can this be garbage, semi auto at you..., burner to the side of your dome, come outta my throne. I've got this locked since 91, I am the truest...."
–Nas Ethor

Ameed had to fight himself to pull his eyes from the Asian girl's small, but nicely shaped ass as her petite 5'5, 110 pounds frame went through the door. He'd met Di 'Wu while spending time in Chinatown and this was the first night she'd let him take her out. How he had chosen Club Prime Time H2O, he couldn't say, but the club itself was off Coventon Highway. Gina and TJ had bought it from the previous owner but decided to keep the name since it already had a good reputation and it brought in good business. The logic was that there wasn't any sense in making unnecessary changes.

Upon entering the club behind Di 'Wu, Ameed took a moment to let his eyes adjust to the lighting. The club was packed for sure, but then too, tonight was *Ladies Night*. Tonight, women got in for half price and only paid half price for drinks.

He followed behind Di 'Wu as she moved through the crowd and found a table near the back. Along the way a light skinned female, who looked like she was in her glass a bit, grabbed his arm and stopped him.

"Damn, handsome. By a lady a drink?" she asked.

Ameed smiled at her.

"My bad, love, but I don't think my lady friend would appreciate the disrespect." He nodded to where Di 'Wu had stop to glance back.

The girl looked at Di 'Wu and it almost seemed like she wanted to say something, but she didn't, instead she pushed on to the next guy.

They had no sooner reached the table when Judah's 5'10, brown skinned frame emerged. "Yo. What's going on, dude?" he asked with his own date holding onto his arm. "How you doing, Di? Oh and I'd like you both to meet Robyn. Robyn, this is Ameed and Di 'Wu."

Everyone traded pleasantries, then they all took seats at the table. Judah jumped up and went to get a bottle of Chablis and then they all poured up drinks to enjoy.

* * *

"Ay, Lee-Lee, look here, Shawty. I've got a job for you and ya boy," Cutt called out as he leaned out the window. He'd just pulled up into Kirkwood, which was known to have some serious Gangsta niggaz in it. Since he already knew that Lee-Lee and his partner, Miles, took up hits from time to time, he'd been looking for them.

"What kinda job, Shawty?" Lee-Lee asked as he walked up to Cutt's truck. He was 5'10, just over 180lbs and dark skinned. At one point in time Lee-Lee played basketball in high school and could've gone to college, but that was before he started shooting heroin into his veins. Now he was pretty heavy into nearly all drugs and even smoked the yams.

"I need you and yo boy to get at this nigga Judah for me. There's two grand in it for you," Cutt told him.

"Judah, ain't that the nigga you used to get money wit', Shawty?" Like everybody else, he knew that Cutt was a slimy ass nigga. He just hadn't realized that he was *that* slimy, but to him, business was business.

"Yeah. So what? Two grand don't care who a nigga is. Do you?" Cutt asked him in a serious tone of voice.

"Nah, Shawty, I could care less. That's yo peoples, but hey, for two grand I'd take yo grandma out."

Cutt smiled. *"Damn right,"* he thought. He grabbed the rolls of money off the dashboard and tossed them to Lee-Lee. With a smile on his face, Lee-Lee asked where he could find Judah. Cutt told him then started his truck and left.

For a minute Lee-Lee stood on the corner thinking. He knew that these dope boys and so-called street niggaz weren't shit. They were no better than him where integrity counted. Especially this nigga Cutt, which he could remember from back when he first came home from prison. This nigga Cutt and Judah were doing it big together. Everybody in the hood talked like these niggaz were *too* rich. Even when they parted ways there didn't seem to be any beef, niggaz still saw them pulling up on one another. But now, out of the blue, this nigga, Cutt, just put a hit out on the nigga. The shit was crazy. Niggaz smile in your face, but really be on the snake shit. Sideways niggaz.

Then again, who was he to talk? He wasn't about to break bread evenly with Miles. He was cool and all that, Lee-Lee thought he could give him 500 for putting in some work, but Miles wasn't going do nothing but smoke the shit up. The nigga had the toughest set of lungs in the city. Smoke a whole yam if you let him. *"Nah,"* Lee-Lee thought. *"Won't be no even cut that's for sure."*

* * *

Jen pulled into the carwash that was down from Glenwood parks. She reached over and turned the music down.

"Hey, I was listening to that," Crystal protested.

"I know. But y'all lazy asses gone help me wash and clean out my truck. So, let's get started," Jen told both of them.

She put the money into the slot then drove the truck through. The drive thru was a little longer than she thought it would be, but Jen spent the time sending a few texts back and forth with Tony. He was asking her if she wanted to spend Valentine's Day with him.

* * *

When Baby Kirk stepped into the house, he saw Sosa and one of his partners sitting in front of the TV playing *Need for Speed* on the PS2. He didn't stop to kick it, he twisted up his face in disappointment though. He couldn't believe this nigga done let another nigga get on his ass about a hoe. He was almost tempted to tell the nigga to go back out there and not to come home until he straightened his face up.

Baby Kirk walked into the bed room and tossed the gym bag on the bed, his girl, DC, looked up. She'd been laying across the bed, looking at something on TV. They called her DC not because she was from the state, but because her name was Dinah Clark and she was a dope boy's princess.

"Yo. Count that for me, Shawty, I'm about to take a shower right quick," he told her.

He didn't stop to wait for an answer, right now his mind was on this shit the white boy at Auto Zone had been telling him. Some shit about niggaz trying to extort him on the hot parts play. The white boy didn't know what to do, but whoever these clowns were, they didn't realize that it was also a part of Baby Kirk's hustle. The white boy swapped parts and the parts coming from Georgia were coming from Baby Kirk and his crew. Now he needed to find out who these M&A muthafuckas really were.

* * *

Lee-Lee watched as Judah parked the Escalade in the parking lot of the Super 8, got out and walked half a mile to another trap. Which made sense, because he wasn't a dope boy and wasn't trying to have the DEA watching his ride like that. All them bastards needed was probable cause these days. Niggaz in the hood had seen just about every trick they could pull. So, the dope boys now tried to think a little swifter. The Super 8 was a trap too, but it was also a business.

None of that even mattered to Lee-Lee. His main thing at the moment was putting two or three hot ones into this nigga when he came back. He'd let CSI figure everything else out.

Judah turned into Glenwood Parks, where the person he needed to see hung out at. He spotted Phat sitting on the hood of a Buick Regal, about to light up a blunt.

"That nigga Budha. I mean, Judah. What's up, Shawty?" Phat asked.

Judah stepped close and gave him a pound. "Phat, what it is, baby?" Judah said. "I see you got yo girl hooked up. Business must be good."

Phat lit the blunt while Judah praised his ride. He'd just pulled it out of the shop two days ago, having hit it with a nice candy paint job, complete with a nice set of rims. "It is what it is, Shawty. Good or bad, I ain't mad as long as I can get my half of the bag," Phat rapped.

Judah shook his head. "Man, I still say niggaz like you should be off in somebody's studio, putting it down. Not out here in the streets."

It was a known fact that Phat had skills when it came to the rap game. On a few occasions he had even done opening shows for some of the major rappers. Two even tried to sign him to their upcoming labels, but Phat always said the same thing.

"Shawty, who gone hold down the streets? You know I'ma hood nigga, so I do's mine the way a hood nigga do his time. But yo, I appreciate the compliment."

Judah smiled as Phat dug into his pocket and pulled out a large roll of bills, which he tossed to him. "I'ma need some more sometime tomorrow. You gone be doing something?"

"You know this ain't no serious hustle, bruh. I've got a job now, but you can text me and see what's up," Judah replied.

"A'ight, Shawty, I'll check in," Phat called out. He watched as Judah walked away, thinking that he really did like the niggah. With the city being flooded with fuck niggaz and lames, a solid nigga could only breathe easy when there were other solid niggaz around.

On a good note, Judah was thinking that today would be a good day. After separating himself from Cutt going to prison and coming home, meeting his sister's future baby's father was a blessing.

Judah bent the corner and was almost to his truck when out of the corner of his eye he saw a sudden movement. He couldn't say why he ducked down but for some reason, he did. There seem to be a voice in his head speaking to him and it shouted for him to drop to the ground ASAP. Judah's entire body went down to the pavement in one motion and as soon as he hit it he heard.

Boom! Boom! Boom!

The window on the car he'd just ducked in front of shattered like ice and Judah rolled until he was nearly under the next car. Then another set of shots went off and another one of the cars windows shattered. This time Judah knew where the shooter was, but still couldn't make it to the Escalade without being shot, so he waited.

47

After a minute had gone by, he looked under the cars and saw a set of feet moving towards him. He glanced around, looking for a way to move without being seen, but it didn't look too likely. The only way that he was making it to the Escalade would be a mad dash, which wasn't 100%.

Just when he didn't think there was a way out, Judah heard the scream of tires and loud music. When he was about to look out, he heard a number of shots. Then a moment of silence.

"Ayo, Budha, you a'ight, Shawty?"

"Yeah. I'm good," he said as he pushed up and saw Phat standing in the door of his regal with a Glock in hand, watching as a smoke grey, Daytona Charger pulled off.

"At first, I didn't know what was going on," Phat said as Judah walked over to where he stood. "I heard the shots and when I looked, I didn't see you. I just saw this crackhead nigga standing there aiming a gun. Yo, shit serious. Shawty, you got smokers shootin at you," Phat proclaimed.

Judah looked at him funny. "Crack head. What he looks like?" He then listened as Phat described Lee-Lee to the tee.

"Shawty, you know that nigga?" Phat asked.

"Yeah, the nigga originally from Simpson Rd. He takes up hits from time to time. The question is, who the fuck would put a hit on me? Lee-Lee ain't stupid, he knows my MO." Judah became silent in thought.

"Shit, Shawty, what's up. You need some back up? You know I've got these killers riding shot gun with me," Phat said.

But Judah shook his head. He knew that Phat's team was all dope boys and gang bangers. What he didn't want to do was tie himself into any street shit. These days niggaz help you today and you owe 'em a kidney next week. Fuck if that was about to happen.

Judah thanked Phat for coming through in a clutch situation like that. Then he made it to his truck and got inside. He still couldn't figure out who would be stupid enough to put a hit out on him. He seriously couldn't remember having beef with anybody. Kool was the only nigga known to use Lee-Lee and Miles on a regular basis.

* * *

Lee-Lee drove like a mad Russian. He was still pissed off. That hit should have gone down different than that but that fuckin Regal had surprised him. The shit came from out of nowhere and then this other nigga jumped out waving a fucking gun like the A-Team. Now the shit was all fucked up and he knew it too. This nigga Judah would damn sure be out looking for him now. The nigga in the Regal had seen his face and then there was this nigga Cutt, Lee-Lee didn't do refunds.

Ameed sat inside of the office thinking about his next move. This white boy at Auto Zone must have assumed they were frontin' because he hadn't been able to catch up with him since. Just then the intercom buzzed on the desk.

"Yes," Ameed asked.

"Mr. Blacksun, there are two FBI agents here to see you. They say you'll want to speak with them," his secretary said.

What the fuck? "Yeah. Please show them in." Ameed was trying to figure out where he had slipped. Did this white boy run to the cops on him? And if he did, what the fuck did he tell them? And just when he thought that he was about to have an epiphany his door opened and he looked up to see Agents Simkins and Flowers enter the office.

"Agent Simkins," Ameed said. "I thought we were good with you. Something else must've happened." He watched as the older Blackman glanced around.

"I really came to see your partner, Merrick. Is he around?" Agent Simkins asked.

"Nah, he uh moved to Atlantic City, N.J. He's getting into the casino business," Ameed explained and watched as Agent Simkins smiled.

"Muthafucka!" He cursed. Then he turned to Agent Flowers. "Didn't I tell ya I like that guy?"

Ameed watched as she nodded and for some reason that Ameed didn't understand, Agent Flowers winked at him.

Trai'Quan

Chapter Six

"Street Dreams are made of these, niggaz push beamers and 400E's, a drug dealers' destiny is reachin a key, everybody's lookin for something..."
--Nas Street Dreams 1995.

May 2010

"You're probably wondering why I brought you out here," Louis Sirrelli stated.

He'd just stepped up on deck of the Catamaran, which was a pretty big Yacht. The boat was 67ft in length, a little over 31 ft. of beam. The LOA was 66'6", while the LWL was 61'4". The beam was 31'2". It had two state rooms, both with Queen sized beds and there were two engines; 110hp Volvo's. The entire boat, which was white, coated a good $2,150,000. But to Sirrelli, two million wasn't big money, it was more like pocket change. Especially when considering the fact that, as the Atlantic City Boss, he was currently worth approximately $563 million.

Merrick looked up from where he'd been sitting on deck, next to Monk. At the moment, Monk was casting a fishing line. He'd already caught one nice sized fish but let it go because he wanted to catch something bigger. Merrick could care less; his focus was on the island that sat in the distance. They were technically in the North Tyrrhenian Sea and the island was Corsica.

"What you did spoke of a sincere loyalty to me," Sirrelli said as he stood, gazing out at the island. "Most Italians find it hard to trust Blacks and it's because we feel that the slave lifestyle that was forced onto blacks took something from them," he explained. "But you have two very different blood lines in-

side of you and neither are the blood lines of slaves, I understand this. Even when others will only see your skin and Judge
you by it, me," Sirrelli tapped his chest. "I judge a man's ways
and actions."

Merrick glanced up at the older Sicilian. The older man
hadn't asked Merrick to put the old tycoon out of his misery.
That had been a decision Merrick made on his own. Just as the
decision to stay in Texas for two weeks until the younger Mr.
Jefferson and his lawyer sat down and made it legal in a contract. Mr. Sirrelli owned 20% of his stock so that he could receive finances from it. Sirrelli saw that as a gift. Because it was
both unasked for and unexpected.

"You move like your Corsican blood," Sirrelli said.

Merrick looked down into his hands where he held a cigar
that Sirrelli had given him earlier. He decided to re-light it and
did.

"Most men do things only when I ask them to do it. But a
man in my position sometimes needs men who will do some
things without being asked," Sirrelli said.

Inside of Merrick's mind, Baltasar Gracian spoke up, *"Do
everything pleasant yourself, everything unpleasant you do
through third parties."* He paused in his speech to make sure
that he held Merrick's attention. He then added, *"All men make
mistakes, but the wise conceal the blunders they make, while
fools make them public."*

Gracian was a philosopher who was long dead, but his wisdom was written in the 48 Laws of Power and Merrick studied
from that book often enough to hear the words like they were
spoken directly to him.

"I should have gotten my lawyers to draw up a contract from
the start. But I didn't and you've corrected my mistake." With
that said Mr. Sirrelli gave him a slight nod then he turned and
went back into the cabin of the boat.

For a few minutes after he left, Merrick sat there thinking. Then he turned to find Monk watching him. "Do me a favor, keep your eyes on that guy at all times." He watched as Monk smiled.

* * *

Andretti *Andy* Luis watched as the entire building was being remodeled. Even standing there watching it, he couldn't believe that a black guy had that much money. Well, it had to be a lot, he thought as he watched Berry speak with the Construction Foreman. These being the very best contractors in New Jersey State, the same ones who built 60% of the fanciest and most successful casino's and hotels in Atlantic City. Contractors that Andy knew he would have never been able to retain.

Merrick had deposited the amount of 20 million dollars into an account, but the account was only accessible by himself and Berry. The money was so that Berry could ensure the building received the very best face lift and would be able to compete with the finest on the Atlantic City strip.

Andy shook himself out of his thoughts as Berry walked over to where he stood.

"You wanted to see me, Mr. Luis?" Berry asked.

"Yes, I just left the 5th floor and it seemed that the last two rooms on the East wing were receiving some rather specific modifications," Andy stated while looking directly at Berry, "With what I saw. No one short of a State Senator will be able to afford the rooms."

"I understand your concerns, sir," Berry began. "However, neither one of those rooms will ever be rented out."

This caused Andy to become vexed in thought.

"Oh, and pray, tell, why not?" He asked.

"Well, Mr. Blacksun has decided that both he and his bodyguard will be living in the Hotel," Berry explained to him. "Thus, those specific modifications are his personal requests Sir."

When he finished speaking Berry watched Andretti's face closely. He had mentioned to Merrick that he wouldn't like the idea, but with Merrick now holding 54% of the business interest and he'd invested 20 million in to it from the start. Also, he had somehow earned the respect of the Atlantic City Boss, which meant there really wasn't anything Andretti could do but accept the changes and move on.

Berry was, on the other hand, thinking that these new changes were about to take the Cattani to the next level. New management seem to be what was needed. But he knew there would be a problem between Merrick and Andretti soon and for some reason, he didn't think that Andretti was going to come out on top of the situation.

At the same time, Andretti was trying to figure out how he could get rid of Merrick Blacksun. He had finally come to realize that this guy wasn't planning to leave. Especially after investing 20 million into a business that, at one point, was drinking money. They would still have to draw a large crowd in order to turn a profit and he knew this building hadn't seen a large crowd since before he and Vinnie took ownership of it. So, if it became popular now, he would never be able to get complete ownership from this nigger and that was a problem.

When Merrick saw her, he knew that there was going to be a problem and that was mostly because at the same moment that he noticed her, she noticed him. They were back in Siena, in the countryside were Louis Sirrelli had what could be considered a town. All of which he claimed belonged to him. Every house, business and the lands they were on, he owned it all and all of the people who lived in the town were relatives of his.

What struck Merrick as a surprise was that as he and Monk walked through the downtown area, he noticed that they weren't the only people with dark skin.

When they stopped at one of the fruit stands, he saw her. It didn't really make any sense because Merrick told himself, he was into dark skinned women, real dark skinned. But this woman was nowhere near dark as he liked. In fact, had he not been so close to her, he wouldn't have been able to see the melanin she possessed. But she was defiantly Italian, almost like an Italian with a permanent tan and she held his attention.

When Merrick reached out for the strange looking fruit, she also happened to reach for it, causing them to both grasp the same fruit.

"Oh, my bad," he said as he pulled his hand away, leaving her with a smile.

"No, you should take it, you'll like it. It's an Italian apricot."

He wanted to ask her about *her* apricots, but that wasn't the right thing to say. The girl was tall, that was one of the things that held his attention. She stood about 5'11" and had such a small waist line. She could almost be called petite but she looked as if she had nice hips too. The dress she wore didn't emphasis her shape. He did see that her eyes were a light enough brown to be thought of as golden and her smile, he liked the way she smiled.

"Hi, I'm Merrick." He held his hand out.

The girl blushed. But shook his hand in return. "Nice to meet you, Merrick. I'm Anna."

"So, do you live near the square?"

"I, uhm. Guess you could say that," Anna returned. Then she looked closer at him. "You're not from around here, are you?"

"Not really." Merrick looked back to where Monk stood. Always the watchful eye. "I'm from the United States. A business associate of mine brought me here for a visit." He watched her smile again. This time he could see that she had dimples and he liked those, too.

* * *

"I don't really know Andretti all that well on a personal level," Sirrelli was in the process of explaining. They were seated in front of a fireplace, watching the flames as they danced to their own tune. "But, what I do know is that he's not high in standing with me. You see with me, I take everything with a grain of salt. When I first came into the position as *Head of the Gaming Society*, I came in with the words of wisdom spoken by Baltasar Gracian." Sirrelli reached over to the arm table and lifted his glass which held Conjure and ice in it. He took a sip. "Gracian had certain views on politics, the same as Niccolo' Machiavelli. But one of the things that Baltasar said was, *'Do not commit yourself to anybody or anything, for that is to be a slave, slave to every man. Above all, keep yourself free of commitments and obligations, they are the devices of another to get you into his power,'*" he quoted.

While Merrick listened and learned, he wasn't completely oblivious to the teachings of either Gracian or Machiavelli. He and Ameed had practically deciphered and digested every word mentioned in Robert Greene's 48 Laws of Power. So, while Sirrelli spoke, trying to impress him, Merrick was thinking of the 4th law the entire time. *Always say less than necessary.* Which actually went with the third law, *Conceal your intentions.*

"Mr. Sirrelli. I need to ask you about something. It's a change of the subject though," he stated and saw that he had the older man's attention completely.

"What seems to be the problem?" Sirrelli asked.

"Earlier today, I met this girl in the market place and we shared a few words." Merrick paused in his speech. He was also remembering the girl and her smile. "I think we both liked one another but the problem is, she's Italian. While I think she's a dark Italian, I could be wrong," he explained.

"So, this girl, she's young?"

"I think eighteen or nineteen" Merrick guessed.

Sirrelli nodded his head but then thought about the issue a moment. "This young girl, tell me her name and if she comes from a respected family. I shall speak with them on your behalf," he stated. "But understand this, my young friend, good Italian women are not for frolic, they are for building families together. So, are you sure you want me to speak with this family?"

Merrick took a moment to think it over. Could he really say that this girl liked him the same way that he liked her?

Sirrelli entered the small house that sat on the out skirts of the town. It was a nice house, but too small a place for as large a family that lived in it. There were four girls and five boys to the family, along with the father and mother. The house was only built for a family of four or five. With more than that, they had to sleep crowded, but such was the ways of life sometimes.

"Ah, Don Sirrelli. To what do I owe the honor?"

"Milan," Sirrelli hugged his second cousin on his mother's side." How have you been?"

Milan Giovanni released the Don and stepped back. He hadn't seen his cousin standing inside of his house since their Great Grand Papa passed away. He was very curious as to why Don Sirrelli wound be here now. "Please, cousin, have a seat."

Sirrelli noticed his wife, Julia, looking into the room from the kitchen. The sons, he knew, were all grown except one. The girls, except the one he was there to ask about, were all under age.

"Dear, cousin. How is the fruit farming?" Sirrelli asked.

Milan smiled. "Oh, it's alright. The boys pretty much run it these days. My oldest, Michael, has control of it. Sometimes my oldest girl runs it," Milan's words stopped as he realized that Don Sirrelli was distracted at this point. "What is it, cousin? Surely my Anna did nothing disrespectful."

"Ah. No, no. Actually, it's quite the opposite," Sirrelli said.

Milan gave him a funny look. At seventy-one years, surely Don Sirrelli was too old to want a young wife. One too young to be tied in with an old man.

Sirrelli noticed the look. "No, cousin. Tis not me who's been captivated by her beauty. I haven't seen her since she was but a child." He laughed, but noticed how Milan sighed, he truly wanted his daughter to be happy one day and that happiness would not come at the hands of an old Don.

"Then who is it that is infatuated with the child?" Milan asked.

He listened as Don Sirrelli explained the situation to him. What Don Sirrelli said was understandable. Especially the part about the young man's blood line and then there was the promised dowry the Don was offering, if it came to a wedding.

* * *

Anna Giovanni did remember the guy from the fruit stand and she had enjoyed their conversation. But she hadn't realized that he had ties to Don Sirrelli, nor had she realized how great his interest was in her. While she would admit that he was attractive.

"Marriage, Papa? Are you sure?" She didn't think this guy was that much interested. Yet she could be wrong.

"Yes, girl. But Don Sirrelli has assured me this will not be a forced marriage. This is your choice and the dowry being offered is truly respectful. Worthy of a Queen," Milan explained. "So obviously you have impressed a wealthy young gentleman. One in his business circle."

Anna allowed herself to smile. She hadn't thought that he was wealthy, he wasn't much older than she was. Maybe it had been family wealth and maybe it was this wealth that caused her father to overlook the fact that Merrick was black, which wasn't really a problem to her, Anna didn't see life in colors. Plus, she'd learned their history in concerns to Hannibal's invasion when she was young.

"Papa, will this dowry help the family?"

"Child. This dowry will make me a Don," Milan told her. "It also includes a business investment. One where our family will eventually become wealthy. Never before have we been in such a position," he explained.

Anna nodded. She knew they had always been poor and suspected they would always be poor. So, if by this union, her family would benefit, then so be it.

Trai'Quan

Chapter Seven

*"... (I'm out the hood)... And if you feel me put your hands up...
(Hood)... My hood niggaz gone and stand up... (I'm so hood)...
And if you not from here you can walk it out and you not hood
if you don't know what I'm talkin' 'bout."*
--DJ Khalid I'm so hood

Cutt Throat was sitting in the barber's chair at the Glenwood Barbershop, getting his hair cut. He was getting a low-cut fade when Judah walked in. Before that moment he'd been having a pretty good day, his money was right, he'd just bought a 2009 Escalade; he wasn't quite ready to get the 2010 yet. He wore an $ 1100.00 outfit, with at least $ 3000 in jewelry.

His whole demeanor changed when Judah walked in wearing Tru Religion jeans, a NY Giants jersey and a fitted hat with some forces. Cutt Throat was thinking this nigga made hood shit look better than what he had on.

"That nigga Judah. What's up, Shawty?" Cutt asked as if he truly meant it.

"Everything's real, bruh. What's up, Dino, can I get a cut?" Judah asked.

When Dino told him to take a seat, Cutt's eyes followed him all the way to the barber's chair. *This nigga, Lee-Lee done missed, now I can't find his bitch ass.* Cutt thought.

"Word on the streets is you got yo self some problems, Shawty."

"Yeah." Judah nodded. "Some stupid muthafucka done sent Lee-Lee at me. But whoever did it really got a lot in common wit' dat crack head. They both some bitches," he said, as Dino tied the apron around his neck.

Cutt damn near came up out of his chair and got directly on this niggas ass right then and there. But he wasn't stupid, he'd heard this nigga was learning some kung Fu shit from that rich nigga he was hanging with. "Shit, Shawty. All you gotta do is say the word and I'm there. Believe that, Shawty," Cutt said.

"Nah, it's cool," Judah replied. "I've got that nigga Lee-Lee in hiding. But I ain't gone chase his bitch ass. He'll pop up. And when he do...."

"Yeah, but you know that. Shawty works for the check," Cutt told him. "What about who ever signed it?"

"Can't do much about that. Lee-Lee most likely ain't gone rat on the nigga, so I'm a dead that ass." Judah leveled his head so that Dino could get at the top. "But there's one thing I do know."

"What's that, Shawty?" Cutt asked.

"Putting a hit on *me*, that ain't cheap, which means this bitch ass nigga gone try it again. Somewhere down the line, I'll get his ass too," Judah said with a passion.

Cutt kept his thoughts to himself. He really wanted to shoot Lee-Lee himself because he had fucked the lick up. But it didn't matter. He realized that he was talking to a dead man. Judah just hadn't gotten the news yet.

While he continued to cut Judah's hair, Dino couldn't help wondering if Judah suspected Cutt Throat for being the one that put the hit out on him. Shit, *he* suspected him. Especially after seeing the look on his face as they spoke. But Dino wasn't no fool, so he kept his mouth shut.

Stepping outside of the barbershop after his cut, Judah saw Cutt hop into the 2009 Escalade. Nice ride, he thought, but he already knew that Cutt got it because he had one.

Walking over to his own Escalade, he thought about how he almost accepted Cutt's offer to help. The whole thing about fucking with that nigga again wasn't cool. That and Ameed wouldn't approve of the street hook up at all. It really didn't matter anyway. He'd just gotten a lead, another crackhead told

63

him that Lee-Lee might be hiding out over on Line street. She'd even mentioned that he had some family over that way. He just had to figure out how he was gone go about this business.

* * *

Ameed stepped off the elevator and walked down the hall, toward his office. There were several other businesses on that same floor.

"What's good, Janice?" he asked his Secretary as he approached.

She was dark skinned, about 5 '5", with a nice body, from what he could see. Julius kept using these Nation of Islam women, so a person really couldn't lust like that. "Hello, Mr. Blacksun. Nice suit," she commented. "Oh, and your brother called. He said call him when you get a chance. He said it wasn't important. But call any way."

"A'ight, I appreciate it," he replied as he stepped into his office.

He hadn't spoken to Merrick in about two months now, but he did know that he was having the casino that M and A Corporation's now owned 54% of, remodeled. It seemed the casino was in poor shape, too poor for it to turn them a nice profit. So, Merrick financed the new face lift it was receiving.

The last time he'd spoken with Merrick was to let him know that these FBI agents were still watching him, why he didn't know. He sat behind his desk, hit a few buttons on his computer and the financial statements came up. So far it showed that between the limo service, the percentage in the law firm, Princess' escort service and the bail bondsman business, they were doing really good. Of course, that was not to include all of the extortion fees money and the money that they made from the weed and pills. They were above the expected.

Ameed still hadn't gotten past the Auto Zone deal yet. He'd spoken with Princess about it and what she suggested might work. It seemed this white boy wasn't scared of the Cops, which meant he might be paying them. Ever since that deal with the guns they took, the ATF screaming that those people worked for them, Merrick said they needed to be a little more careful. They hadn't realized that these crooked business men were dealing with the cops and since the ATF wanted their shit back, they'd given them all of the guns and stolen parts. Merrick told them they destroyed the dope, which almost caused a conflict but they came out of it without having to lose.

So, he couldn't risk putting too much pressure on this white boy at Auto Zone. Other than that, Ameed had his financial team looking into another investment. He was thinking about buying a club and the club he wanted was O'Reily's on Coventon HWY. If they could get that, then business really would pick up.

* * *

Agent Simkins rolled over and reached for the pack of cigarettes that were on the bed side table. This was the first time he had ever been inside of the Marriott. He used his lighter to put fire to the end of the cigarette, behind him Agent Flowers was still asleep. The day before yesterday was the first time he'd ever put his dick into her and he wasn't complaining.

He swung his legs over the side of the bed, stood up and walked to the bathroom to take a piss. He stood at the toilet with his head back, enjoying the release. When he was finished, he shook it off then stepped over to the sink and washed his hands. While doing so, he looked at his reflection in the mirror on the wall and thought about his life as it stood.

He was forty-eight years old, with twenty years on the job. They mostly gave him those cases that they couldn't solve and out of every ten, he was sure to bring four to a close. His track record was just that good, four out of ten was damn good considering the fact that any other agent might not get one. If they were lucky, they would get just that, one.

Simkins looked at himself and wondered what good it really did. He didn't have anything to show for it and the world damn sure wasn't a better place. He sighed and blew smoke at his reflection. Something had changed in the last year and a half and he knew when. It all started with that Miami heist, with this guy, Merrick Blacksun.

Simkins wasn't a dirty cop. He wasn't even tempted by those things that made other cops dirty. He was just trying to do his part, but there was something about this guy Merrick that kept pulling at him. He suspected strongly that Merrick pulled the heist, even if the evidence said something else. Nobody could fake their finger prints. Yet he knew that somehow everything tied in to this guy. Most importantly, he was impressed by the way that this guy moved, which was why they were still in Atlanta. He really wanted to see if this guy was as sharp as he appeared to be.

He tossed the cigarette butt into the toilet and flushed it. He wondered what his own son would have been like had he lived. He would have been twenty now, just a year younger than Merrick.

Simkins turned and left the bathroom.

* * *

Jen did everything she could not to let them get to her, but she still saw them as soon as she stepped out of the school. Sosa and three more of his boys had been hanging around her school a lot these days.

"Girl, maybe you should tell one of your brothers," Monica advised.

"Yeah, cause this nigga is asking for it." Crystal added.

Both were walking with her as they headed to student parking. Jen felt the same way, it was defiantly bait. Sosa wanted to bump heads with Ameed again and she suspected he would have a gun or something this time.

"Don't worry about it." Jen smiled. "We've got three more weeks until graduation and then Snipes will be here."

They both knew that she called her older brother Snipes and both Monica and Crystal were thinking that if what Ameed did to Sosa wasn't shit, then what would Snipes do?

* * *

"Mr. Blacksun there's a guy here to see you. He says his name is Smith and that you'll want to see him," the secretary said.

Ameed knew who Smith was, the guy from Auto Zone. But he wasn't expecting to see him. "Yeah. You can send him in," he said anyway.

"Uh, sir, he brought another guy with him," she added.

"A'ight. Send them in."

Maybe the guy had changed his mind or something. At least that's what Ameed was thinking when his secretary opened the door and let the two men in. The white guy he expected, but not the black guy, who must have thought he was a rapper or something. He was wearing baggy jeans, Roca wear shirt, Air-max's and jewelry, along with an Atlanta Falcon fitted hat.

Ameed stood up to greet both men. "Mr. Smith, and who might your friend be?"

"Actually bruh, I'm his business partna," the black guy interjected." My name's James Datsun, but most people around my way call me Baby Kirk."

Ameed then sized the dope boy up. If he wasn't mistaken, Judah had mentioned this dude. He was supposed to be that little punk who was bothering Jen's uncle or something.

"Business partner, huh?" Ameed said. "Which would mean that Mr. Smith here told you about the offer I made him." Ameed retook his seat and waved for both of them to have a seat in the chairs across from his desk.

"I explained to my business partner," Mr. Smith began. "That you approached me with an offer. But that I was already doing business with someone who couldn't entertain the proposition."

Ameed laced his fingers together in front of him and looked over at the two men sitting in front of him. "So, what exactly is your purpose for coming here, if it wasn't to discuss business?"

"Actually, Shawty, I wanted to meet you," Baby Kirk put in. "I been hearing about your company all over the A. So, when my man told me you were trying to get in on the hustle. I had to think about it. So, now I'm thinking that maybe we could do something, Shawty."

Ameed looked at him for a moment, actually seeing how stupid these poorly educated dope boys made black people look. He sighed. "First of all, don't call me Shawty." He looked straight into the other man's eyes when he spoke. "I'm from New York. We call women and kids shorty and I'm neither. I don't care how you country bumpkins try to freak it, the shit means the same thing. In other words, it's disrespectful and disrespect will be dealt with. Understood?" Ameed watched as the older, black man struggle inside with the reality in front of him. "Second of all you misunderstood, we never offered to do business with *you*! We merely offered our protection for the business Mr. Smith does." Ameed then looked at the white guy. "Really? You brought a drug dealer to my office as your back up?" He watched Smith hunch his shoulders.

"Wait a minute, Shaw, uh, bruh." Baby Kirk caught himself. "It don't matter what type of business a nigga get started in. That's just to get his feet wet. I'm trying to get into some legal shit like you got going on here. I bet you had to hustle to get here, so why you frowning on me?"

Ameed shook his head. "Bruh, I've never sold crack, cocaine or any other hard drug, a day in my life. So, don't compare yourself to me," he stated. "And for the record, M and A Corporation don't do business with drug dealers. I mean, how stupid could that be? We put our name on a dope boy and he gets busted. Then the Feds come and take our shit. Nigga, please, you watch too much TV."

"Hold up, bruh." Baby Kirk felt violated now. "I understand you got your thing going on here, but you ain't about to be talking to me sideways. Nigga, my name ain't whispered in the streets, Niggaz know me and respect me so...,"

Ameed held his hand up. "Listen, let's be real. The only *real* difference between Atlanta and Augusta is bigger buildings, you slimy ass niggaz and the six letters following the A. I've seen niggaz in Augusta who could run circles around you niggaz. So, don't come up in my office flexin' about who you are. That shit doesn't even begin to impress me."

"A'ight, I'd like to see a nigga from the country out hustle me," Baby Kirk said.

"Don't tempt me," Ameed told him.

"I could flood your whole trap with thugs and have you so-called city niggaz rethinking whose country, you or them."

With that, Ameed changed his focus and looked at the white guy. "Look, we hadn't realized that you had this type of drama going on and like I said, we don't deal with drug dealers. So, you can forget the offer. From this point on, neither of you will have to worry about M and A Corporation and with that said, good day gentlemen."

For a minute, no one moved. Prides had been checked and Ameed could tell that they were both in their feelings. He watched as they stood, then made their way out the door.

At the door, Baby Kirk stopped and glanced back once more, then he stepped out. Ameed knew he was going to have to deal with the chump eventually. He just had to find a better way to do it. One that wouldn't connect back to the company.

Trai'Quan

Chapter Eight

"I want a Villa in Costa Rica, where I can smoke my reefer and enjoy how life's supposed to treat you. Laid in the shades of the Everglades, finally forever paid, wearing the finest fabric's tailors have ever made..."
AZ--- Sugar Hill

"Yeah, I'ma be there the week of the graduation. I might even bring my new lady friend," Merrick spoke into the phone. He glanced over to where Anna and Monk were sitting on deck. Talking, Merrick hadn't thought Monk wouldn't talk to anybody but him. Yet for some reason, he would talk to Anna with no problem. "You talk to the old man lately? Well, tell him I'll get at him when I get back into the states. Yeah, yeah. Okay, look I'm about to go. But I love you, so take care."

He ended the call then looked out across the waters. Sirrelli had given him the use of the Yacht so that he could spend some time with Anna and as a safety precaution her father insisted that her brother Juan come along with them. At the moment, Juan was rolling a blunt as he sat next to him.

"So, what's it like in the states?" Juan asked. He finished rolling the blunt, then using a lighter, lit it and in hailed deeply.

"I don't really know how to explain it," Merrick told him as he accepted the blunt.

"A lot of different things could be said, but you'd really have to see it to understand it," he explained.

Juan accepted the blunt back. "I kinda wish that I could, but we have no family in the States," he said.

Merrick knew about the dowry that Sirrelli was offering their family if him and Anna did decide to marry. That and the business investment where he was petitioning to make their father a Don.

"Tell you what," Merrick said. "In about two weeks we're flying back to the states for a week. My baby sister is graduating high school. How would you and Anna like to come?"

"Are you serious?" Juan asked.

Merrick understood the logic. If he wanted to spend time with Anna before they married, it would have to be with a family member present. Besides, he liked Juan. The boy was only sixteen but mature for his age. He hadn't been able to finish school himself, because they'd been too poor and he had to join his brothers in the family business.

* * *

"So, what exactly do you do for business?" Anna asked.

They were back at her family's farm and at the moment they were sitting in the twin swings, outside, talking. Her mother made it a point to keep them in her line of vision from the kitchen window.

"I built this company with my best friend and we have several things that we're into. Different investments."

"And this company is how you met Don Sirrelli?"

"In a way. I bought half of a casino from a guy and before I could step in as part owner, I had to get approval from Mr. Sirrelli."

They were silent a moment. Her younger sisters were also out there but they weren't bothering them, they were playing while they talked.

"Why is it you have no wife in the states," she asked, because she really wanted to understand. Here was a handsome, young man who had both money and power. Yet he had no wife or kids?

"There was someone last year, but she passed away. I've been single ever since. I guess it would be safe to say that only certain types of women can catch my attention."

She thought carefully over that answer. "In a woman, what exactly do you look for?"

"Intelligence and a quick wit. I like sharp women, who can keep up with me."

"I don't think that I'm that smart. I only made it to the eighth year in my school."

There was another moment of silence.

"If you could, would you have liked to finish?"

"Yes. But education here costs a lot of money and when you're poor, you can't get free schooling," she explained.

"Tell me, what would you like to be? If you could be anything you wanted."

Anna thought about the question seriously. "I come from a large family and we're very close. I would like to have a large family of my own one day."

Merrick thought about Jen and how it was just them. He once had a step brother, but that was another story. "I would like a big family myself." He smiled and watched her sisters playing. He was remembering his step brother.

* * *

"So, what do you think?" Merrick asked.

Both he and Monk were sitting in the back seat of the car as they rode back to the Villa.

"She's a good girl," Monk told him. "She'll make a good mother and she'll be loyal to the right man."

Merrick thought about that, he agreed. Mostly because he was thinking the same thing. He had asked if both Anna and

Juan could spend the week in the states for his sister's graduation and their father had said it wasn't a problem, as long as she and Juan shared the same room. The truth was, he wasn't about to do anything disrespectful any way. He was really serious about this.

Monk was actually wondering how many people suspected the truth. It hadn't taken him long to figure it out and since he'd been around, it didn't look like anyone else had caught on. When he was in the army, he had seen something like it before, but not quite like this. With Merrick, it was too controlled, even he allowed himself to show his anger. A person would have to be looking really close to see the actual change and Monk had seen it several times now. Yet he didn't think that either one of them knew he'd figured it out and he wasn't about to say anything.

Merrick had been having the headaches again. He'd taken enough pain pills to put down a horse, but he curled up on the bed holding his head anyway. It had never been this bad before, usually only gaps in his memory and a slight headache. Ever since the day he received the news of Tammy and Kenya's deaths, it had been getting worse and then there was the other thing. Merrick was wondering if Monk had noticed, he couldn't be sure. He would have to be more careful in the future.

* * *

Sirrelli had allowed them the use of his personal jet, which was an International Lear. The jet landed at Hartsfield/Jackson International airport. Once it was on the ground it taxied up the runway and eventually came to a stop. There was a stretched Range Rover limousine sitting not far away. The door opened and the stairs came down.

The first person off of the plane was Monk, followed by Juan and then Anna. He led them both to the limo while their bags were being off loaded and brought to the limo as well. Merrick was the last one off, having stopped to have a word with the pilots.

Since he and Monk had moved to New Jersey, they'd both let go of the leases on their condos. Being the case, the limo drove to the new house that his mom was living in, out in Lawrenceville. The house itself was two stories, 2,620 sq. feet. It had four bedrooms and three baths and he had paid $215,000.00 for it.

As soon as the limo stopped and the door opened, Jen was the first one out of the house. She jumped in to Merrick's arms. "I missed you, Snipes."

"Yeah, I missed you, too, Jen." He hugged her. "But, hey, I want you to meet someone." Merrick turned and waved for Anna and Juan to step out of the limo. Anna walked over and stood next to him. "Anna, this is my baby sister, Jen. Jen this is Anna," he introduced. "Why don't you take her inside and show her to a room. Me, Monk and Juan are going to check in with Ameed."

"Alright. Come on, Anna." Jen took her hand and pulled her to the house.

Merrick smiled at her as Anna glanced backwards but they soon vanished into the house. Once that was taken care of, he returned to the limo with Juan.

Judah drove up Candler Rd. as in his mind he was still thinking. He hit Glenwood and drove a minute, made the left by Texaco and proceeded to Line Street. The crack head had told him that if he was lucky, he would find a Daytona Charger parked in one of the driveways. If he saw it, then Lee-Lee would be around.

Slowing the black Ford Expedition that he was driving for the job he thought he could have just as easily paid somebody else to tighten his ass up. But he kinda took this whole hit on him thing kind of personal. That and this nigga had been hiding for almost three months. Judah wanted to make sure that this nigga got it. Besides, he needed to see what this new Sig-Neuhausan 9mm P-210 was working with.

* * *

Damn, two grand didn't last no time, Lee-Lee thought as he brought the shooter up and lit the end with the lighter. Of course, he'd had help smoking it. This bitch Pam helped and she was smoking like *she* had the fuckin' dope. *Bitch done smoked more dope then me*, he thought as his lungs filled with the smoke and the pipe got hot, beginning to burn his fingers. He was starting to think that he would have come out better smoking with Miles. But, nah, that nigga had deep lungs. Plus, he'd fucked Pam twice already and was gone fuck her again. The bitch had some good pussy, or was that the dope talking? Either way, being cooped up in one area for too long had the dope playing tricks on him. He couldn't take the chance that he'd run into that nigga, Judah. The way he saw it, he'd just wait until the nigga let his guard down, then he'd see about that ass. Shit, he wasn't in no rush, the nigga, Cutt, ain't said it was on no dead line and if he started trippin', Lee-Lee was thinking, *I'll see about his shiesty ass, too.*

"Damn," he spat, the lighter had gone out. He tried to flick it but it wouldn't strike. "Now ain't that a bitch?"

"Nigga, don't be calling me no bitch! The fuck you think you is? You don't know me like that." Pam was rocking back and forth on the sofa until she heard that.

"Nah, not you. The damn lighter went dead."

She focused her eyes and watched as he kept trying to get it to light. Finally, he gave up, dug into his pocket and pulled out two $5.00 bills and started to hand them to Pam to tell her to go buy some lighters. *Some good ones*, he thought. *Nah! The bitch might pocket the money and get caught trying to steal them.* "I'll be back. I 'ma run up to the store right fast," he told her.

"Just hurry back." Pam's eyes focused on the half ounce lying on the coffee table. "My nerves shot. I'ma need me a hit in a minute."

You always need a fuckin' hit, he thought as he stood up and grabbed his jacket. *Might as well get something to eat while I'm up there.*

* * *

"Tough ass nigga." Judah said to himself. He just looked up and saw the nigga materialized in the street but he didn't get into his ride. Instead, he took off on foot. Nine times out of ten he would be going up to the store for something. Judah slid the clip out of his gun and checked it then pushed it back in. "'Bout time I tighten this nigga up!" he mumbled.

* * *

Lee-Lee flicked the lighter a few times as he walked out of the parking lot, heading back to Line Street. He'd already checked it inside the store, before paying for it so he knew that it worked, but kept telling himself that a cheap lighter could go out at any moment, so he kept checking to make sure.

In his other arm, he carried a brown paper bag with a few other items in it, some food and snacks he'd seen inside. Other than that, his only thought was of smoking this dope. He was so focused that he wasn't even paying attention when the dark SUV pulled up beside him.

"Say, bruh. You live around here?" The voice from inside the truck called out.

Lee-Lee glanced up. He couldn't really see the person's face, especially at this angle. "Yeah, something like that," he said not even recognizing the fact that he couldn't see the guy he was talking to. "Why, you lost or something?" For some reason he got a funny feeling, almost like Deja vu.

"Sort of. I'm trying to find this nigga I was supposed to meet at this address," the person in the truck said. "Here look."

Not thinking twice about it, Lee-Lee turned and stepped closer to the truck. When he saw the barrel of the gun his whole body froze up and he looked into the guy's eyes for just a split second. Lee-Lee knew that it was the dope that had him slipping, but it was just too late, so he held his breath and took it like a man.

Boom! Boom! Boom!

The 9mm jumped each time in Judah's hand. He watched as the three slugs half lifted Lee-Lee's body and threw him backwards. The brown bag went in the other direction and the lighter just dropped to the ground. Judah watched for a minute as the body flopped like a fish out of water.

"Pussy ass nigga," he said before he pulled off.

"Oooohhh," Not far away, Pam flinched with each shot as she heard them. She already knew what it was about, seeing as she was the one who told Judah that he could find Lee-Lee on Line Street in the first place.

"Oh, well." She dug into her pocket and pulled out another lighter, which she didn't tell that fool she had. Then she reached for the half ounce and the razor that was on the coffee table. "Might as well put this to good use," she said. Without a care in the world, she started smoking.

* * *

Agent Simkins was sitting at a desk in the GBI building, looking over all the latest reports. What he was really looking for was war crimes that were like the ones where the ATF's were bumping heads with Merrick. He'd had to pull Agent Beats aside and explain to him that this guy Merrick was a suspect in an ongoing Federal investigation. It seemed the ATF were beefing with Merrick about some drugs that they never got back.

What Agent Simkins didn't tell them was that the cop that was murdered in Augusta Georgia with his family and the drugs the DEA found, were most likely theirs. He also didn't tell them that this Cop was on his list of suspects for the Miami heist, or that the GBI agents found at the scene were all assigned to his unit. Some deep gut feeling told him their deaths had nothing to do with the drugs that were found at the scene. Agent Simkins told them just enough to make them back off Merrick. Now he had to see what would happen next.

Trai'Quan

Chapter Nine

"I grew up on the crime side, the New York time side, where staying alive was no jive... At second hand, moms bounced on all men, until we moved to Shao -and- Lin...."
Wu Tang Clan –CREAM '94

"What? Nah, thug. Nigga, don't make me come way over there and fuck you up about that little piece of change. Is yo life worth so little?" Cat-Eye looked at both Snipes and Ameed as he listened to the fool on the other end of the phone running his lip. Although he was hearing this clown, he was thinking about what Snipes had just asked him.

They were standing in the back of River Glen, in the parking lot. Snipes and Ameed had pulled up in a Royal blue 2010 Camaro and parked next to his 2010 GMC Suburban. *Twenty thugs*, Cat-eye thought. Yeah, he knew twenty thugs who would follow his instructions, but were these two niggaz serious? Cat-eye had never been a big dope boy in the game, he damn sure wouldn't have thought he could be the brick man.

"Look, nigga, I tell you what. Don't have that check when I come through. Nah, Nah, keep poppin' that killer shit. I like it when niggaz talk stupid." He ended the call, then looked at the two men before him. "So, how you gone do all of that? If I take twenty thugs up to the *A*, I'm going to have to be sure these niggaz can eat, on a regular basis."

"Listen," Snipes said. "You just get your team together. Ameed will make Sure you get enough cocaine to let all of them eat. This is his thing."

Cat-eye glanced around the projects. One thing he knew about these two, they didn't play games. "Tell you what, How about y'all run me over here to Hell Street Apartment's right quick. This nigga, Crazy, think I'm playing."

Snipes looked at Ameed since this was his business in the first place. He still wasn't about to get into the drug business, but he understood what Ameed was about to do.

"A'ight. Come on," Ameed said.

* * *

Hell Street was always jumpin'. The business was almost as good as it was down on East Boundary, and Crazy was defiantly getting his share. He stepped up to the Nissan that pulled in to the parking lot and bent down to the window. He made the sale then walked back to stand with his crew.

The whole apartment complex was a dope trap and there were so many niggaz out that sometimes it was a fight just to catch a sale. Crazy had a whole lot going on at the time and then this nigga wanna call and trip about some punk ass weed. The shit wasn't that good anyway.

He made another sale then it came back to his mind what Cat-eye said on the phone about his life being worth a little. Subconsciously he reached behind him and touched the .45 that was tucked into his back, in the waist band of his jeans. "I wish that nigga would," he said to himself. No sooner had the words left his mouth than they heard the loud music beating down the block.

"Look what I got, an ole school, a truck and a drop, so next time you think ya peeps on top, Shawty look at da squad, got respect from the killaz and G's, so next time you think them niggaz is G's you probably lookin' at me..."

Crazy watched the Camaro pull up with the TI playing, sitting on 22-inch rims. The music was still playing as the car pulled up and stopped right in the center of the parking lot. No one got out and to Crazy, it felt like someone had walked over his grave. He shivered and goose bumps popped up on his arms.

The door opened and he watched Cat-eye step out with a sawed-off Mossberg pump, pistol grip. Behind him he saw both Merrick and Ameed and at that moment, Crazy realized this nigga was fuckin with them two.

"Oh! Shit!" He shouted but it was already too late. The most he was able to do was turn and try his best to get the gun out.

Kha Chink Boom!

The first shot tore the left side of his waist out and he started losing all feeling at once.

"Oohhh!"

Kha Chink Boom!

The pump spoke a second time, as if it couldn't get enough of the conversation. His right thigh was hit and pushed out from under him. Somehow, he kept from falling but the .45 hit the ground and slid away from him. "Aaah," he moaned

Kha Chink Boom!

The shot tore into his back and all sound coming from him stopped. Everyone watched as his body froze for a split second then he fell face first, like a tree.

Cat-eye stood there and glanced around, but it looked like everybody was minding their own business and trying to look everywhere else, except at him. He turned back to the Camaro where Merrick and Ameed stood. "Yeah, I'll come up to the *A*. Especially if you gone put some bricks in my hand," he said.

"Oh, one other thing," Ameed said. "How about you bring that pump with you?"

Cat-eye smiled and held the shotgun up. "Keisha? Man, I don't leave home without her, anyway. Ain't no telling when a nigga gone get tired of living."

* * *

"So, what's up? You want it or not?" T-RU asked from where he sat behind the wheel of his blood red, Chevy 1500, which had 24-inch chrome rims on it. At the moment he was talking to this nigga Tyrone, who stood next to the truck, while over in the passenger seat Gangsta, his partner, was rolling a blunt.

"I like your numbers, bruh," Tyrone said. "But right now, all a nigga can get is four of them gents. Not nine. If you can hit me wit' that this trip, I can get my weight up."

T-RU sat in thought for a minute. He then reached over and pressed the lighter in. When it popped out, he used it to light the cherry flavored Black and mild. Him being Piru, he did everything bloody.

"Tell you what," he looked at Tyrone. "I usually give niggaz at least one chance to show they true colors, before I dub em. So, I'm a fuck wit you thug, but it's on you to hit back."

He took the money Tyrone handed him and then passed him the package. With the deal completed, he started the truck and they pulled out of Barton Village.

Not long after, he pulled into Meadow Brook. T-RU had just turned onto the street when he saw the Camaro in his sister's drive way, but what caught his attention was the two niggaz standing next to it. T-RU pulled up next to the car and parked. Then he and Gangsta got out.

"I didn't think you thugs came to the hood anymore," he said.

"Nah, only when it's necessary," Ameed replied as they did a fist bump.

T-RU was Patrice's cousin, so he knew who they were. He also knew that they had moved to Atlanta last year.

"I heard you niggaz were rich now a days," T-RU stated.

"Nah, we just living," Ameed said. "But look, I've got a job for you."

He took the next five minutes to explain what he had in mind and how he wanted to put it into motion.

"Can it be homies?" T-RU asked. "Cause not all of them are from the spot."

"It really don't matter to me, as long as they rep. the Thug Life. Besides, I did some homework. There's a lot of Bloods in the area I'm sending you to," Ameed explained. "But I'm a need you to support Cat-eye and his thugs, too. They gone be in another area."

"Fo' sho, my nigga. Fo' sho," T-RU smiled. "And you gone put the work in my hands?"

"You and thug," Ameed said. "When y'all touch down I'm a hit y'all both with ten bricks each. We ain't worried about the bread. I just need control of the streets. So, all of the money you make, y'all keep."

"Say no mo' Dawg. We gone bark at you in about a week," T-RU informed him.

Ten keys to basically move these country niggas out of Ameed s way. Shit, T-RU was thinking. That was a whole lot of dawg food and he and his set was about to put everybody on the plate...

* * *

"What's really going on, bruh?" Ameed asked as he drove.

"What you mean?" Merrick shook himself out of his thoughts.

"You've been spaced out since you came back. What's really up? Something I should know about?"

Ameed whipped in and out of traffic. Coming off the 15th street over pass, he made the necessary turns to get on to Wrightsboro road.

"Been thinking about this," Merrick said.

When Ameed looked over, he saw him holding a two and a half ct. diamond ring, encased in platinum.

"Whoa! Is that what I think it is? You thinking about commitments?" Ameed asked.

"Yeah, I guess that situation with Kenya and Tammy sort of fucked with my head," Merrick said. "I think, I think the loss of them and the two seeds messed with my head somehow. Now all I can think of is wanting my own family."

"Fuck! And you gotta get married to do that?" Ameed asked. He was about to have a baby with Princess and was trying to put one in to Di'wu. But he wasn't trying to be locked into no commitments.

"Not really, but love is Sicilian and with the way these people move, ain't nothing happening without a ring. Plus, I have these feelings for her and then there's the fact that Monk talks to her."

"Damn, that nigga talks to somebody other than you?" Ameed was surprised. He'd just hit I-20 and was now driving them back to Atlanta. It would be late when they got back. "Listen, son. I guess that I can understand. I mean you've lost a lot since we started this and niggaz just want something that they can call they own. But, yo, on the one," Ameed glanced over at him and for a minute he could have sworn that both of Merrick's eyes were green. It wasn't the first time he'd thought that, but he always assumed it was a trick of the light, so he brushed it aside.

"But what?"

"Oh, yeah," Ameed continued. "If you serious about this, then, bruh, you can't have no wife mixed up in this street shit. You should have learned that already. You can't have her where your enemies can get to her. So, you gone have to think about that."

He was thinking about it. Well, one part of him was. That emotional part, the part that cared the most. Merrick knew that he couldn't handle losing again and there was a part of himself that wasn't about to accept that kind of loss ever again.

* * *

"So, Anna, you're Merrick's girlfriend, huh?" Crystal asked.

Jen shook her head as she drove while over in the passenger's seat Anna didn't seem to be offended by the question.

"Uh, I guess that's what you would call it here," Anna said.

She was enjoying spending time with Merrick's sister, who seemed to want to drive her all over Atlanta in her Denali. Jen kept taking her shopping.

At first, Anna wasn't sure what to do when Merrick gave her his black card, but then Jen started to buy all kinds of clothes and reminded her that Merrick said she could have whatever she wanted. The past three days she'd hardly seen Merrick, but then, too, she knew that he was busy with his business partner. The first day she'd only bought two Chanel outfits and a Fendi bag, which she told Merrick about when he asked.

Anna was surprised when he asked, "Is that all?" He'd then turned to Jen and said. "Take her out again and make sure she buys everything she looks at."

So now Anna had everything from Ferragano and Gucci, to Sergio-Valente and Donna Karen and Jen was still telling her to buy more stuff.

"So, what do you call it where you from?" Crystal asked.

Both she and Monica were riding in the back seat. All of them would be graduating in two days.

"Where I'm from, it's called espousal or betrothal," she explained.

"Wait a minute. That means engaged right?" Crystal asked.

"Alright, that's enough questions," Jen interrupted and she saw Anna smile. Jen already knew what was going on between her and Merrick. The more time she spent with Anna the more she liked her and was looking forward to having her as a sister-in-law.

* * *

He didn't always take someone with him everywhere he went. So, when he found himself standing over the three graves by himself, Merrick wasn't surprised.

"I kinda wish that I could speak to both of you face to face, I mean, there's a lot that I want to tell you. Things that I feel I need to explain." He paused for a moment before continuing. "Some of it I don't even understand myself."

He was squatted down between both Kenya and Tammy's graves. "Something's wrong with my mind. I mean," the wind was blowing around him and it was getting dark out since they'd gotten back to Atlanta after 6:00. But he wanted to do this before he placed the ring on Anna's finger

"It's like there's two of me sometimes. The me that's emotional and open to this love or caring about thing. Then there's the one who's sort of like the Incredible Hulk. I don't mean big and green, but there are times when I'm always angry and the funny thing is, on the surface it'll never show, but sometimes, sometimes I don't even feel like I'm in control. That's the part I really don't understand because I can actually see everything that's going on. It's almost like I'm watching a movie." He fell silent.

Merrick really didn't know how to put it all into words. For some reason, while in thought, he looked up and to his right. That's when he saw the figure walking towards him. Merrick's whole demeanor changed as he stood, starting to reach into his trench coat for his gun.

"Hold up, cowboy, I just want to talk to you," the guy said as he came closer.

Ameed had told him that this guy had been hanging around lately. "Agent Simkins? It's kinda late to be hanging out in a grave yard isn't it?"

He watched as Agent Simkins smiled. Showing off the one, open face, gold tooth and his neatly trimmed goatee. "Are you sure you want me to answer that? I mean, I'm not the only muthafucka out here, am I? If I didn't know any better, I'd say you were having a conversation with a couple of head stones."

Merrick smiled back. "Nah, you ain't got to answer. So, do you want to tell me why you're really following me?"

"Other than the fact that I know you got away with $100 million dollars, of somebody else's money, killed a lot of crooked cops, bumped heads with the ATF and somehow beat the FBI data base computer." Agent Simkins looked at him closely.

"Nah, I don't remember doing any of that stuff, Agent Simkins. Must have been a guy with my same MO," Merrick said.

Agent Simkins laughed. "Muthafucka, you wanna go get a drink? I'm off the clock, so right now I'm not an FBI agent."

"As long as I'm not drinking with a cop," Merrick replied.

"Defiantly *not* a cop," Simkins told him.

Trai'Quan

Chapter Ten

Although one half of me is man, the other half amazes me.... Because, that half of me that's man, is the half that keeps me grounded in these streets. While that which is amazing wants to push me above and beyond my natural potential... Together they form the necessary reality inside of me.—Merrick, the natural birth'

Agent Simkins took Merrick to the Maruge Club on Glenwood, where they got a table in the back and a bottle of Conjure, with two glasses.

"Been a long time since I sat down and had a drink with a muthafucka who wasn't a cop," Simkins said.

"Yeah." Merrick looked across the table at him while he brought his glass up and took a sip. "Just as long as you know the difference between being real and being a Rat!"

"Haven't you ever heard that even cops don't like rats?" Simkins laughed.

Merrick watched as he pulled out a box of Black & Mild's. He opened it and shook one out then proceeded to roll it back and forth between his fingers, taking all of the tobacco out. When he had it emptied out, he pulled the brown paper out of the inside and repacked about a quarter of it with tobacco.

Merrick was surprised when he stopped, reached inside his coat and pulled out what looked like an ounce of weed.

"Since neither one of us is a cop, nor a rat." Simkins smiled then began to alternate putting weed then tobacco into the cigar until it was filled up completely.

"You ain't got to worry about a piss test?" Merrick asked.

"Probably. If somebody ever suggested that I was a crooked cop," Simkins said as he lit the cigar. "But hey, ain't nothing crooked about me." He in hailed deeply off the cigar then he coughed a few times, choked some and then hit it again. "Damn, I see why they call that bitch Irene," he said.

"You do know you sort of act like Denzel did in Training Day, right?" Merrick asked.

Simkins laughed. "Can you believe the bullshit? Them bastards waited for brother man to play a crooked cop before they gave him an Oscar. Now how disrespectful is that? Why not give him one for Glory, or Malcolm X?"

"They actually did the same shit with Hali Berry in Monsters ball," Merrick added.

"Sidney Poitier, he had to play the part of an Uncle Tom Negro," Simkins added. He held the cigar out for Merrick who took it and toked.

"It seems like blacks only get noticed when they degrade themselves," he said as he smoked.

"Yeah, ain't that a bitch?"

Merrick handed the cigar back to him then asked, "So, seriously, you're not a crooked cop?"

He watched as Simkins inhaled deeply again, then held the smoke in for a while before releasing it.

"That depends on how you define crooked." Simkins replied. "If you mean like Denzel was in the movie. Nah, I'm not crooked. I'm not a killer and I don't steal drugs from drug dealers." He passed the cigar back. "But do I get high and drink a little Cognac. Hell Yeah."

Merrick hit the cigar, deep in his thoughts. The cigar was shorter now, so he gave it back. "You take bribes?"

"Hell no! That would defiantly make me a crooked cop," Simkins stated. "But, hey, everybody likes gifts. Shit isn't a bribe and a bribe isn't a bribe when the money isn't used to seduce favors."

Merrick gave that some thought. He poured himself another drink, pulled out a pack of Newport's and shook one out. "So, somebody gives you a, say a nice watch, for something like Father's Day, which is this Sunday. It's just a gift, huh?"

"Yep, just a gift," Simkins said. He watched as Merrick removed the $2500 Cartier watch that had twelve diamonds in it and placed it on the table in the middle.

"You got kids?" Merrick asked.

"Had a son. Would have been about a year younger than you right about now." Simkins looked in to his glass. "I was living in Chicago then; my boy was only thirteen when some Gangster Disciples killed him because he wouldn't join their gang. I guess that's why I frown on the black on black crime angle the way I do. Now a days I guess you could say I live for the job more. But since I'm retiring soon, hey," he hunched his shoulders.

Merrick was listening to the story, but most importantly he listened to the man. Hearing his pain and understanding it. "I just lost two kids before they could even be born. So, I guess I can feel your pain. Mine still hurts me, too."

"The two graves? I read about it."

"Yeah." Merrick leaned forward and pushed the watch across the table to him. "Happy Father's Day."

Agent Simkins lifted the watch and looked at it. He could tell that it was expensive. He'd never owned anything like it before, the job just didn't pay like that. He removed the cheap Timex that he wore and put on the gift. "You know, in the Bible, it's been spoken of Angels that had personal dealings with man. Some of these Angel's became guardians of men, protector's if you will. Do you know what the best part about all of this was?" He was still looking at the watch as he spoke. "Neither the Angel nor the men asked one another for a thing. There was just an understanding."

Merrick smiled. "Yeah, that which is understood, needs not to be explained." He watched as Simkins reached into his pocket and withdrew a piece of paper. He slid it across the table to him. Merrick unfolded it and looked. There was a name, address and phone number on it.

"My sister, Jackie. We don't have the same last name, we have the same father, different mother. She has a son, Kenny, he'll be in the 12th grade next semester. Wants to go to college and be a lawyer but nobody in our family makes George Town money. If my sister could get him into that school, man, a brother who was committing white collar crimes could go a long way when the right people turn their heads." He reached out for Merrick's cigarettes. "You mind?"

"Nah, you good," Merrick said. He understood everything that was being said and that which wasn't being said.

Merrick woke up at dawn the next day, which really wasn't much sleep since he'd only slept two hours. He brushed his teeth, took a shower and by the time everyone else got up he was already started. He cooked breakfast and set the table. When his mom, Jen, Anna, Monk and Juan were all seated he walked over to Anna and held the black box out to her.

"Ohh!" His mom expressed.

Merrick watched as Anna opened the box and removed the ring. She handed it to him and he placed it on her finger. Anna stood up and wrapped her arms around his neck as she kissed him.

When the kiss broke, he said, "Can you put the wedding together in three months?"

"I'm not sure. That's a lot of work and money and people to invite," she told him.

"I would like to have it here in America and I would like to bring my family over, but...."

Merrick placed a finger over her lips, then looked at Jen. "Baby girl, you willing to help?"

"Of course." Jen smiled.

"Then don't worry about the money," he told Anna. "And if you want, you can move your whole family here permanently. You about to be my wife and that means as long as your loyal to me, there's very little that you can't have."

He watched as Anna nodded her head with tears in her eyes. He didn't tell her that he'd already made adjustments to the dowry. He had already told Sirrelli that he wanted to move her family to the States and had Sirrelli looking for a large enough house in New Jersey for them. If not that, then he would move to Georgia. That way neither Anna nor Juan would have to go back to Italy. They just hadn't been told that yet.

* * *

Jen graduated with honors and the party that her brother threw her was incredible. All of her friends and family came and then Snipes surprised her by telling her that she could attend any college that she chose. She decided to put that on hold until after the wedding.

* * *

"Who was that nigga in the Excursion?" Merrick asked.

He was standing outside with Ameed when he saw the truck ride by his mom's house with the tough guy leaning out the window, mean mugging Ameed like they had beef.

"That's the nigga I told you about, the one stalking Jen. He's the dope boy's nephew," Ameed explained.

Merrick watched as the truck turned the corner, leaving their line of vision. "Is he a problem? Because I'm not taking any more losses with my family." His eyes were still looking up the street.

"Nah, I'm already planning to let T-RU handle that as soon as they pull up in Kirkwood," Ameed told him. "The nigga might have three weeks of oxygen left in him."

To which Merrick nodded, he wasn't about to see any more of his people gunned down for free. The old rule was, they didn't deal with the streets, didn't sell drugs and so on. That was the old rule. The new rule was, Ameed would run Georgia and to do that he needed to control the streets. So, Ameed sat down and explained his plan, that the Chinese had the dope and all he needed to do was put two men into position, thus keeping himself out of the dope game but in control of it.

Since he was using niggaz from the spot, Merrick told him, "Hey, this is you, baby. You rock it the way you want to, just be smart about it. I'll be in New Jersey running my Casino."

In other words, as long as it didn't come back to the company, Merrick wasn't going to get in the way. And now that he saw this nigga stalking Jen, he really didn't have a problem with what Ameed was putting into motion for Kirkwood and Edgewood. Both of them were close together so T-RU would be able to use Cat-eye if he needed him, because Cat-eye wasn't affiliated.

* * *

"Ayo, Peace, God. They just called your name for visit."

Richardo looked up as his student Cee Truth stuck his head in the door. He'd just finished getting dressed and hit himself off with the Dolce and Gabbana blue. He'd paid one of the female guards to bring it in. "How I look?"

"Man, you one hunnid," Cee Truth told him.

"A'ight, hold this while I'm gone." Richardo handed him the phone. "If my Earth calls, tell her I'm in V-I. My kids came for Father's Day."

He'd eventually pulled one of the female CO's, her name was Dyniesha Reeves and for a short woman she was on point with her small waist and large hips. The best part to him was that she was half his age, had him feeling like he was twenty-three again.

* * *

"Happy Father's Day, Pop," Merrick said. He hugged his old man then stepped back while Jen gave him a hug.

Richardo turned his attention to Anna when Merrick told him that he was getting married in three months. He was happy for him. When Merrick told him that she was Italian, he was kind of conflicted. As a Five Percenter, he knew the history of Italy, he knew that quite a bit of them had melanin in them. He could tell that she did, just from looking at her. "And this is my future daughter in law. Welcome to the family."

"Thank you," Anna said.

Richardo hugged her and then they all sat down to enjoy the visit. He hadn't seen Merrick in a while because he'd been busy with his business.

"Oh, Pop, remind me to tell you about this cat named Randolph Stevens before I leave," Merrick said.

They talked about other things, mostly Richardo asked Anna a lot of questions and he saw that she and Jen were pretty close. Merrick made mention of the fact that he had a business idea for him. When he came home, Merrick was thinking about starting another limousine service, this one in Atlantic City. He'd already checked and while they had several already, there never seemed to be too many. The thought was maybe they would do something like that.

"Oh, yeah and who would I be working for?" Richardo asked.

Merrick smiled. "You work for yourself. M and A will only own 15% of your business, the rest is yours. You hire and fire who you want, but it's also a float or sink business deal," Merrick explained. "I'll have everything set up for you when you get out but it's on you to make it work and to keep it working."

Richardo thought about it. Shit, how could he not keep it working? Only an idiot would mess something like that up and it would be legal.

On the way back, they were all in the Denali that Jen drove. Merrick was in the back seat, stretched out sleeping. He'd driven all the way there so now Jen was driving back home.

"I like your father," Anna said.

Randolph Stevens, Richardo, sat in his room thinking about what Merrick told him. Apparently, he had someone in the FBI and they'd found out that the rat was living in Canton Ohio, working at the post office. The nigga had a whole life: wife, kids, everything and here he was doing all this time because that nigga ate the cheese.

Richardo smiled as he pulled Canton Ohio up on his iPhone and read about the small city. Yeah, that was the best Father's Day gift Merrick could have given him and he was going to enjoy it the first chance he got. But for now, he was going to savor it. One thing was for sure, he was defiantly going to deal with the rat.

Chapter Eleven

"The rat, The cat, The snake, The dog, How you gone see em when you living in the fog?" –DMX Damon

One week before the wedding

"In physiological terms, it's what we would call Dissociative Identity Disorder or DID and what that means is the individual creates, within his own mind, an alternate personality, another self."

Merrick looked at the doctor from where he sat in the brown leather recliner. "Go ahead , Doc, I'm listening."

"Oh, yes, right." The doctor cleared his throat then continued. "What actually causes the manifestation is often times a case of post-traumatic stress. It's when the individual experience's something traumatic enough to the point where they themselves regress logically from the situation. The true self allows for an alternative self, or type personality, to emerge. This alternative self s usually better able to adapt to and/or deal with, whatever that situation may be. Let's say for instance, a rape victim. The individual may have trouble accepting or adjusting to the situation, especially in times when certain types of men approach them. Thus, triggering the alternate self to take over and in doing so, giving the necessary responses to the situation at hand."

Merrick almost laughed but forced himself to hold it in. "I've never been raped, Doctor, nor sexually abused."

"Oh, of course not. I didn't mean to imply that you had been, I was just trying to explain how these things worked. However, if what you've told me is true, then you must've experienced something. It's a very unusual case where the subconscious mind creates an alter ego without some type of intense trauma. That is, if what you've told me really is the truth."

The doctor paused a moment in thought. Merrick wasn't sure what that thought could have been.

"I have an idea. This may, or may not work but it won't hurt to try. How do you feel about the subject of hypothesis?"

With a serious look on his face, Merrick thought about the question. He really didn't think that stuff worked for real. Only in movies. "You want to hypnotize me? But let's just say that it does work. What happens if I lose control and he, I mean, my alter self, does something that I may regret later."

There was a lot that he really hadn't explained to the doctor. When he first decided to see a shrink about his problem, Merrick had been of two minds about it. One reason was due to all that had happened in the past three months. Things he sometimes couldn't remember doing but knew that he had done them. It was like being inside of a dream sometimes. While on the other hand, he was getting married next week and he wanted to know if he was really crazy or if it was all a dream.

"We'll set up some key words. Safety words. These words will be used to bring your true self back into control and the best part will be that we'll record these sessions. You'll be able to go back and review it on your own time. This way you'll be able to see that which may be inside you, if there really is something inside."

But Merrick already knew something was inside. How else could everything he'd done be explained. He just wasn't sure that this doctor could handle what was there.

As the pendulum rocked from side to side, Merrick focused on the small beam of light. He listened as the doctor counted backwards from one hundred and he felt no different than when they'd first started this experiment.

"I don't know, Doc, I don't think it's working."

"Hmm. Maybe if we continued for say..."

Something twisted inside of Merrick's mind. It seemed as if, at first, there was one beam of light. Then it rippled and split, only it didn't split once, the light split into many different beams, then rippled again and refocused into four beams of light. It then became steady, with no more ripples.

The doctor also witnessed the change. At first, he thought that he was seeing things. He glanced over towards the camcorder to make sure that is was still running then looked closer at this guy. He still couldn't believe that he was really seeing what he thought he was. In all of his sixty-four years, forty of those in Psychiatrist study, research and practice, he had never seen anyone experience both a mental and physical change like this one. This man's eye color literally changed right in front of him. When he first came into the office and before this experiment, the doctor was sure his eyes were a mixture of greyish green with slight traces of brown. Now, as he watched, his eyes went to brownish grey, then greenish brown and amazingly, they ended up as a dark grey, no green and no brown in them.

"Yeah, it's me, Doc. So, what's really good?" The personality asked.

It had a deep New York accent. Earlier the doctor noticed that he sounded like he was from New Jersey.

"Uh, good? I'm not quite sure I follow you."

He was still trying to put together the eye color combination and what it meant. He watched as the guy stood and looked around, taking in the office. He walked over to the window and looked outside. The office was on the 26th floor of a 33-story building.

The doctor watched as he reached in to his jacket, withdrawing a pack of Newport cigarettes and a lighter. He shook one out and looked up at the doctor.

"You mind?"

"Oh, no, not at all. I just didn't think that you smoked."

"Yeah and who signs your check?" He smiled as he lit the cigarette and inhaled deeply. "But I'm not Merrick and you brought me out here, so what seems to be the problem? If there ain't nothing wrong, then, Doc, we might have a problem."

"A problem? Why exactly would we have a problem? Your other self is paying me to speak with you. By the way, what is your name? If you don't mind my asking."

He smiled as he puffed on the cigarette then glanced out the window. "You sure you wanna talk to me, Doc? Or would you like to talk to one of the others? By the way, I'm Mr. Black."

"Others? Merrick seems to think there's only one. How many are there?"

"Besides me and him, there's Snipes and then there's the Boss, Don Omerta. Each one serves his own purpose," Mr. Black said as he put the cigarette out on the window sill. He then walked over towards the desk and said, "You know, for a shrink you don't seem very smart. I mean, no offence, Doc." He picked up a picture frame from the desk and looked at it. "I guess I'm the center of attention right now, since I've been on the scene the most these past three months. So, it's only natural that he'd focus on me. Especially with me being the one that puts in the work."

"Puts in the work? What exactly does that mean?" Somehow he knew he wasn't going to like the answer, even before he asked. Either way, he watched as Mr. Black gave him a funny smile.

"I'm the killer, Doc. That's what I do! That nigga, Snipes, he's the one that deals with all the emotional and romantic shit and Don Omerta is the business man. He's the brains of the whole operation, the one who keeps everyone safe. But I'm the bad guy, Doc and guess what?" he asked in a sinister way.

The doctor watched as Mr. Black reached under his jacket and withdrew the black Glock .40 then pulled out a palm length black tube from his pocket.

"Wha—t are yo—u doing with th—attt?" The doctor stared, petrified as he watched Mr. Black screw the silencer onto the end of the gun.

"What? This? Relax, Doc. I'm not going to kill you. The Boss doesn't want you dead," he said as he placed the gun on the desk then slid his right hip onto the edge of it. He picked the picture up and looked at it. "She's cute, who is she?"

"My—my youngest daughter." The doctor was so afraid that he didn't think he could stop his stuttering.

"Okay, so here's the deal, Doc. You've only got one chance of me walking out of here with you still breathing. All you gotta do is tell me everything you can about your daughter. But, if I feel like you're lying to me," Mr. Black hunched his shoulders and nodded his head to the pistol lying on the desk top.

"Bu—but why?"

"It's really simple, Doc. You see, I don't need the cops showing up on our door step with warrants and shit. I mean, the Don is a smart guy and I'm pretty sure he could get us out of it. Oh, yeah that reminds me." Mr. Black stopped talking and pushed off the desk. He moved over to the camcorder which sat on the tripod, picked it up then slammed it down on the floor. The digital chip popped out and he picked it up, slipping it into his pocket. "Now, then, as I was saying, your daughter is actually your insurance policy, Doc. So, spit it out."

* * *

Merrick shook it off and then looked across to where the doctor sat, shaking off his own fear. There wasn't any need to guess why, he'd watched as it all happened. Now he knew the truth. He looked down and realized that he still held the chip from the camcorder.

"Look, I'm really sorry, Doc. I—" He couldn't even find the right words to explain what Mr. Black had done.

"Could you— could you just leave, please," his voice trembled.

"Yeah. But let me just write you a check." Merrick pulled out his check book and pen. He felt the weight of the Glock .40, with its silencer still on it, inside his shoulder holster. And he damn sure didn't smoke cigarettes, he only smoked weed and a cigar from time to time.

"No, that's alright. You can keep your money. In fact, this session never happened, none of it. I just want you to leave. Leave me in peace and please, God, never come back."

Merrick dropped his head. Truly ashamed by what Mr. Black had just done to this man. "Yeah, okay, Doc."

Merrick watched as the doctor fought his tears. He wanted to say that he was sorry, but knew that wouldn't help the situation. As he stood up, he looked down at the older man who wept over the single photo of his daughter. Merrick knew that the girl was only twenty-four and in college at Princeton. He knew everything about the doctor too. He also knew that the doctor would never tell anyone about Mr. Black because he knew the doctor understood, doing that wasn't safe.

After Merrick left the doctor just sat there. He was astonished. "Amazing, simply amazing," the doctor spoke to himself.

He still found it hard to believe and he'd actually experienced it. Yet there was no proof of it, the video was gone and if he ever told anyone, he knew what would happen to his daughter and he believed it. "Four real personalities inside the same body! Unbelievable."

Merrick got into the forest green 2011 Escalade SRX and started the truck. As soon as he did the CD player selected a song, but when the song began, he knew that it had been the last song that was played. He guessed Mr. Black had been listening to it.

"Now who I am is who I be until I die, either accept it or don't fuck with it but if we gone be dawgs then you stuck with it. Let me go my way but walk with me, see what I see, watch me then talk with me... Share my pain make it a little easier to deal with. Rob and steal with. Dawg nigga what, ride till we die it's on nigga what..."

The CD skipped twice as he sat there actually listening, trying to process the meaning of the words DMX was speaking.

He put the truck into reverse, then looked into the rear-view mirror. One of his eyes was greenish with traces of grey while the other one was brownish with traces of grey. Now it seemed to be a more controlled shift between personalities.

"Yeah, I get the picture," he spoke to the image in the mirror.

He backed up and then pulled out of the parking lot. There were three more months before the year 2011 began and he wasn't exactly sure what kind of year that would be. He was about to open another casino that he'd acquired and his pops would be coming home. This deal he had with the Mafia was still standing and he had three different personalities inside his head.

Merrick thought back to what the doctor had told Mr. Black. *"But, Merrick doesn't need any of you to protect him,"* he had tried to explain.

Mr. Black had laughed. *"Malcolm X once stated I believe in anything that is necessary to correct unjust conditions. I believe in it as long as it's intelligently directed and designed to get results. But I don't believe in getting involved in any kind of political action, or other kind of action, without sitting down and analyzing the possibly of success or failure..."* Mr. Black paused. He looked the doctor in his eyes closely. *"The Boss told me to tell you that. But it serves the purpose, Doc. You see, it doesn't matter what you think. It doesn't even matter if Merrick agrees with you..., the truth of the matter is, me, Snipes and Don Omerta, are all a part of Merrick. We make being Merrick possible. So whatever Merrick has going on, Doc, all of us want in!"*

Chapter Twelve
Everything that happened before the wedding/ After Father's Day

"I need your help." Don Sirrelli looked across the desk to where the other man sat.

He was Italian, too. His name was Paul Peralli' and he was from Staten Island. He wasn't a Don, but he was in high standings with the families. Peralli' ran the docks down on the Hudson and because he did so, he had dealings with more than just the Italians. He dealt with the Russians, Chinese and even the Irish at one time or another.

"What exactly seems to be the problem?" Don Sirrelli asked. He really didn't like getting into the affairs of the New York families. Especially when he controlled Atlantic City.

"It's my son, Donnie," Peralli' began. "He got himself in deep with the Irish. He..." Peralli' paused, not knowing how much he should tell the Atlantic City Don.

"Look, Paul, we're family. You're my wife's third cousin, if I can help you, I will. So, tell me, what did Donnie do?" He watched as Peralli' sighed and wiped sweat off his forehead with a handkerchief.

"The Irish, they say Donnie stole $50,000 from the warehouse and their giving me pressure to return it."

"So, have Donnie give the money back," Don Sirrelli suggested, but even as he said it, he realized that for him to do so would be a problem.

"Donnie's missing," Peralli' said. "And I believe they plan to off whoever brings the money back to the warehouse. The problem, Mr. Sirrelli, is I can pay the money back but you know how the Irish are, they won't let it go like that."

Sirrelli pretty much knew that Donnie was a dead guy, that's if they hadn't already killed him.

"Don Sirrelli, they've threatened my wife and new born daughter," Peralli' added.

This really made the situation worse; the Italians didn't hold a lot of love for the Irish Mafia already. They were too blood thirsty and reckless. The Irish expected everyone to be afraid of them because most of their business was in arms trading, guns.

"They give you a dead line?" Sirrelli asked.

"Five days from today."

Which meant he really had seventy-two hours. Don Sirrelli thought about the situation, he understood why Peralli' didn't go to the New York families with this. His son, Donnie, was the one to transgress first, the Italians wouldn't want a war because a war would mean unnecessary exposure. It would surely be a blood bath because the Irish would feel they had a point to prove. They would also see this as a way to take control of the warehouses and it would be blamed on Peralli'.

"Do you have any idea where Donnie might be?"

"He might be in Brooklyn with some cousins."

Sirrelli nodded. "Go home, Paul. Kiss your child and enjoy your wife."

"But, Don Sirrelli, what about my problem?"

"There is no problem, Paul, but you will owe me a favor one day. For now, just forget about the Irish, I'll speak to someone about it."

* * *

"I want kids, "Merrick stated. He was lying on his back in the park, not far from his mom's house in Lawrenceville, a nice quiet suburban park.

"How many kids?" Anna asked. She was lying next to him in the grass and they were looking up into the clouds. It was a beautiful day outside.

"I don't know. How many will you give me?"

"Well, Sicilians believe in large families and as you can see, I come from a large family. So, I guess it'll be as many as I can give. We'll just have to wait and see," she explained with a smile.

"I guess we'll have to get a big house." He laughed then his Galaxy came to life. Merrick dug into his pocket and pulled it out, seeing that the call was from Sirrelli.

"Mr. Sirrelli."

"I have a problem that I could use your help with."

Merrick sat up and glanced sideways at Anna. She was watching him. "Is it important?"

"I've only got seventy-two hours to solve the problem and it might be real messy. It would mean a lot to both me and my wife if you could help."

Merrick gave it some thought. He already had Sirrelli's support, this was yet another opportunity to get in deeper with him. "It'll take me a while to make the drive."

"That won't be necessary, the jet's still at the airport. I just spoke with the pilot; they'll be ready to leave in the next thirty minutes."

"Alright then, I'm on my way," he ended the call.

He was expecting Anna to say something because this was supposed to be their time, but all she did was smile and nod her head with understanding.

* * *

Ameed stepped out of the stretch Lexus limo as it came to a stop inside the parking lot of Crim High School. When he looked up and saw both Cat-eye and T-RU, he smiled. "Were y'all able to get apartments in the two neighborhoods?"

"Shiiit." Cat-eye laughed. "I just brought my baby mama and gave her enough money to rent the spot. She gone put in for public assistance sometime later, but I'm good thug."

Ameed nodded then looked at T-RU.

"We just pulled up on the Big Homies who were already out there in Kirkwood. It seems like the GD's been eatin' real good out there lately. But when I told them that all the Bloods could eat off our plate, boy you know they got down. We just waiting on you to drop that work, thug."

Again, Ameed nodded then he glanced around the parking lot. All he saw was T-RU's partner, Gangsta, standing next to the 1500 and the two thugs Cat-eye brought with him. Other than that, there was no one else out there.

"Come with me." Ameed turned and led them to the trunk of the limo. From inside the Lexus the driver popped it open. When Ameed lifted the lid, their eyes locked in on twenty kilos of cocaine.

"Boy. Shit. That's what's up!" T-RU exclaimed.

"Hell yeah, I'm the muthafuckin' brick man!" Cat-eye added.

"Tell yo boys to pull up and get ten each. While they do that, I need to explain some things to y'all," Ameed said.

They both told their teams to pull the trucks to the back of the limo. Afterward, Ameed pulled them all back towards the front of the limo. He didn't want anyone else to hear what he had to say to them.

"A'ight. Here's the deal. Me and Snipes, we don't sell dope, so I won't be involved in what you do. The ten bricks is all yours but you gone have to be smart and business minded to make it work. The plug I'm going to give you will sell you keys at 18,000 each. You'll have to have your money right in order to re-up."

"Say no mo'," T-RU said.

"Boy, watch me turn ten bricks into fifty." Cat-eye laughed. Ameed watched them dap one another. "T-RU, Snipes needs a favor from you as soon as you get your homies in order."

"Thug, you two niggaz can get a hundred favors," T-RU stated.

Ameed laughed. "But yo, thug, this shit is personal. There's this nigga that's pushing up on Snipe's baby sister, Jen."

"Hold up. You mean little Jen?" T-RU asked.

Ameed smiled. "Yeah, she ain't but seventeen. There's this nigga who's twenty something and he won't take no for an answer. She ain't into him. I think the nigga on some ole *he got a point to prove* shit. Like he can get whatever he wants when he wants it. So, when she said no, he just isn't hearing her."

"That sounds like these so-called city niggaz. They need a reality check most times."

"Well, after losing Kenya, Snipes ain't taking no chances. So, he needs this nigga out the way. And I need this nigga, Baby Kirk, out of the picture. The whole point of this is to gain control of the streets, which means he's gone be a problem, anyway." Ameed laid it out.

"Nigga, that's it? Shit, thug. For ten bricks, we would have killed every nigga in Kirkwood who ain't homie or Ruby, you know, our female bloods. And you can just tell Snipes them two niggaz just got dubbed out.

* * *

Don Sirrelli looked up as Merrick entered the office followed by Monk and the young boy, Juan. Why he was with them Sirrelli didn't even ask, instead the old man explained to them what the situation was and why it was necessary.

"So, how exactly do you want it handled?" Merrick asked.

"Honestly, the father can give them the money back, but he needs to be reassured that there's no further threat to his family," Sirrelli told him.

"So, whatever you decide, I just need a solution to this problem."

With that said, Merrick, Monk and Juan left while Sirrelli sat there still contemplating. He wasn't sure how this would be handled but for some reason, he felt like it *would* be handled.

* * *

So far, the remodeling of the casino was coming along good. Andretti performed his usual checks, paying special attention to certain areas. But as he moved about, he became aware of a mobile trailer that was parked to the side of the building. The trailer had been there before, he'd noticed it but thought that it was something to do with the construction crew. Now he was seeing a long line of women, most of them looking like models and his curiosity was getting the best of him.

Andretti made his way over to them and once there, he excused himself as he moved to the front of the line. He pushed his way into the trailer and saw Berry sitting behind a desk, looking like he was more important then President Obama.

"What's going on here?" Andretti asked.

Berry looked up from his current interview of a young woman. "Ah, Mr. Luiz. Um,"Berry attempted to speak.

"I asked what was going on here, Berry," he stated and watched as Berry swallowed hard.

"Well, a part of what Mr. Blacksun wanted in upgrades was also newer, younger women to work the casino."

"But we have good workers here already. Loyal workers."

Loyal to you that is, Berry thought. He'd been the one to explain to Merrick that the casino's workers should respect their

Pit Boss and that the current Pit Boss didn't have that respect. The workers here respected Mr. Luiz. They hadn't even respected Vinnie. Berry also suggested that this may have something to do with the money constantly coming up short.

He watched as Andretti glanced around at the women, all of them top of the line. Women who would seek jobs at the other Casino's.

"We don't have the budget to pay these people," Andretti said.

Berry knew that he was intending to discourage the women. He also knew that Andretti didn't know exactly how much money Merrick was putting into the whole project. "Uh, actually we do," he informed Andretti. "Mr. Blacksun figured into the expenses, enough to cover hiring all new staff, even a new Pit Boss. Whom I haven't decided on yet."

"*What?*" Andretti was livid. "This isn't his casino! This is my fuckin'..."

"Wrong again, sir," Berry put in. "You don't have the controlling interest in this casino, Mr. Blacksun does and it's his money that's saving a casino which even Mr. Mendoza knew was doomed. Mr. Blacksun says we're no longer catering to the bums and street urchins. He says Casino Cattani will be exclusive from now on and to be exclusive we've got to hire exclusive staff." Berry waved his hand to indicate the women before him.

"By the way, sir, meet our new Chef, Lady Holiday." He watched as Andretti looked at the young woman.

Ms. Holiday was thirty-eight years old and fresh out of culinary arts school with a Masters in exotic foods. She'd been working at another casino as an assistant chef, to another head chef. Berry was able to lure her away with a better position and higher pay and she was a damn good chef.

"We'll see about this," Andretti turned and stormed out.

When he was gone, Ms. Holiday leaned forward and asked, "Uh, should I be worried about him?"

"I doubt it. He won't even be here when we reopen," Berry told her. "The new owner is currently in the process of buying him out. He just doesn't know it." Berry wondered what Andretti would do when he realized the truth.

Andretti sat inside of his Mercedes Benz, thinking. This guy Blacksun was more of a problem than he realized, but he wasn't in a position to do much about it. Especially with the Casino not bringing in any money the past few years. There really wasn't anything that he could do except get out while he still could.

He pulled out his cellphone and dialed a number.

"Mr. Borges, is the offer you made still on the table? The one for my half of Casino Cattani?"

"Of course, it is my friend, but like I've said, because your other half is owned by this Negro, the price can't be more than what I presented. I'll still have to find a way to deal with this guy," Borges explained.

"Well, that's not my concern. How soon can you have the papers drawn up and the money ready?" Andretti asked.

"Is five days too long for you?" Borges asked.

"No. That's perfect. I'll meet you in five days." Andretti ended the call.

Raymond Borges owned three other successful Casinos in Atlantic City and two in Las Vegas. Andretti was thinking that he would have the money and power that it took to put an end to this guy Blacksun. And even though he wasn't getting as much as he wanted for his half, he would still be comfortable and even satisfied, knowing that Merrick Blacksun would be broken and brought back down to Earth.

Meanwhile, Berry replaced everyone, from the entire cooking staff, to the hotels roster. He also hired all new dealers for the casino and every single one of the new people were women, as instructed by Mr. Blacksun. Now all he needed was to find the right Pit Boss. He understood what Mr. Blacksun was trying to do, the average gambler was male, which meant that they had to keep a lot of eye candy around. The only men Berry was to hire were security and he was also having their uniforms redesigned.

With Berry having been around for a while, having also worked in Vegas, Mr. Blacksun placed Berry in a position to make sure that the Cattani was brought up to the same standards as those casino's in Vegas.

Trai'Quan

Chapter Thirteen

"At night I can't sleep I toss and turn, candle sticks in the dark, visions of bodies being burned.... Four walls closing in on a nigga. I'm paranoid, sleeping with my finger on the trigger... There's somebody watching me at night but I don't know who it is, so I'm watching my back..."
~Ghetto boys, Mind play in tricks on me

"What do you think?" Merrick asked.

All three of them were sitting in the black Range Rover Sport, watching the warehouse and its activities. Two days had gone by and from what they had learned over those days was that these Irish guys were doing a lot of work inside.

"We'll have to kill everybody if we do this the way you want to do it," Monk told him.

"And you're sure you want to bring your student?" Merrick asked, looking up into the rear-view mirror.

In the back-seat Juan was watching the warehouses as intense as they were. Merrick already knew that Monk had been teaching him how to shoot with various weapons and from what Monk told him, Juan was a natural. He said that even his movements were made with incredible stealth and slyness.

"He's ready," Monk said.

Merrick didn't question it. If Monk thought Juan was ready, then he was ready. When he'd first told Merrick that he wanted to train the younger boy, Merrick almost said no. because Juan was about to become his brother in law. But then Monk asked if he knew why Anna's father sent Juan with her as a bodyguard or protector?

"It's because he likes to kill things," Monk had told him.

"What, you mean, like people?" Merrick had asked.

"When I asked him, he said he'd only killed some animals, but I could see it in his eyes. It won't be long before he graduates to larger prey," he'd explained.

That conversation was a few days ago and Merrick had thought about how Monk was spending a lot of time with Juan, showing him how to clean and care for guns, as well as the proper way to use them. Merrick had also seen something inside the boy, a killer instinct.

* * *

"Who the fuck these Blood niggaz is, Shawty?" Sosa asked as he sat in his Excursion with Young Snoop and Glass in the back seat and Big O holding down the passenger seat.

"Shawty, I dunno, Shawty," Big O said in a voice that didn't seem to fit his 6'5" 330 lbs. frame. It was squeaky like that of a young child.

"Shawty, my sista say these niggaz from Augusta, Shawty," Glass put in. "You know, her girl fucks with one of they Big Homies, Shawty."

They all knew that Glass' girl's older sister's friend had a baby by this nigga, Blood Red, who was originally from Monterey, Ca. Blood Red had been living in Kirkwood for almost five years now, trying to get his hustle on. He was never able to get over 18 ounces and he pushed an old school box Chevy.

"Shawty, how many of these Augusta busters they got with 'em, Shawty?" Sosa asked.

Since they were sitting inside the truck, on one of the side streets, watching these niggaz hustle, Sosa was tripping because it looked like these niggaz had some serious weight now. Before, the Bloods didn't have a plug and they usually had to buy work from somebody else, which kept them from growing into

119

a problem. Sosa knew that if they ended up getting a real plug, then they defiantly would become a problem.

"I think they got about ten or fifteen of them niggaz, Shawty," Young Snoop told him. "I ain't seen too many more then that, Shawty."

"Listen, Shawty. We bouts to holla at my uncle." Sosa looked into the back seat. "You two niggaz run over to Kinston and tell the Gangstas over there that we might have a problem. You heard, Shawty?"

"Say no mo', Shawty." Young Snoop opened the back door and he and Glass got out.

"GD folk," he said.

"GD," Sosa replied.

While Sosa was sitting in his Excursion watching the hood, T-RU and Gangsta were parked in the gas station parking lot across the street, watching them. He'd left the 1500 at Blood Reds' apartment and was riding in the 2010 Hummer that Gangsta was driving now.

"See them niggas right there, thug?" Gangsta asked as they watched the two exit the back seat.

"You want me to touch 'em?"

"Nah. Let's stick to the script," T-RU replied.

"The Big Homie Snipes wrote this movie and these niggaz just got cut."

"Foe' sho', my nigga."

"Just chill. I wanna get the two we after at the same damn time." T-RU laughed at his own joke, the reference to the song.

* * *

"Okay. So, what about the DC shipment?" Marcellus asked.

As he listened to his foreman, who was outlining what was going on, he really didn't have any intention of even coming to

the warehouse today. Since Peralli' called saying he was bringing both his son and the money to the warehouse around 7:30,
he wanted to look these idiots in the eyes before he killed them.
He was going to kill the son anyway, for even having the balls
to steal from him. But he just couldn't let the old man live after
that so he was going to let the old man watch first and with the
old man's death, it would serve as a way for them to gain control over the warehouse district. Marcellus was using this viola-
tion as an excuse to kill the Italians and not enter into a war with
the Mafia families behind it. By law, he couldn't just kill the
father without just cause.

He checked the time on his watch. 6:48 p.m.

"Sir, we've just finished drying the last batch," one of the
workers said.

"That would be what, two-hundred thousand?"

"Actually, its two-fifty even, Sir."

"Good. Start packaging it," Marcellus instructed.

That was a quarter of a million going to the DC banks,
which would put them at 42.2 million standing and they still
had enough clean paper to print another seven-hundred and fifty
thousand.

"So, what you wanna do about these niggaz, Unc?" Sosa
asked.

They were standing out in front of Baby Kirk's apartment.
Sosa had just explained the situation with these Augusta niggas
trying to put down but Baby Kirk was remembering what
Ameed had said in the office that day.

"I can't believe this nigga tried me like that, Shawty. He
really brought some country niggaz up here fo' real, Shawty."

"What do we have here now? Do you wanna ride or die?"

The music pumping out of the Hummer as it turned the block was so loud it literally drowned out their conversation.

"What the fuck, Shawty?" Baby Kirk stated when the Hummer came to a completed stop right in the middle of the street. As it sat there, music playing, some of the girls from the projects began to dance like it was a block party or something, until the music suddenly changed.

First off fuck yo bitch and the clique you claim. West side when we ride come equipped with game. Ayo claim to be a playa but I fucked yo wife. We bust on Bad Boys niggaz ride for life...

"This nigga got a hard on for 2 PAC or something?" Big O asked.

As they watched, the doors opened and T-RU stepped out with the chrome plated street sweeper, while Gangsta held the sawed-off double barrel shot gun.

"Ahhh shit Shawty, runnnn!" Sosa screamed.

But it was already too late, T-RU let the street sweeper cut loose with no hesitation. He hit Big O in the chest, throwing him back into the Excursion. Sosa was hit as he turned to break to the left and it seemed to take several shots to bring him down. Baby Kirk on the other hand, wasn't going down without a fight. He pulled out his 9mm and started to bust back. At the same time, some of his other boys ran out into the streets to join in the shootout. They didn't know what was going on, all they knew was two niggaz in ski mask was shooting at Baby Kirk.

Gangsta squeezed triggers and the shells tore through the Excursion as if it was made out of paper. He broke the barrel and reloaded, then once more took aim at the truck because Baby Kirk was hiding behind it. But this time he aimed at the gas tank and squeezed.

Boooom! Boooom!

The shot gun let off.

Kaaah Boom!
The truck itself lifted off all four tires and went up into the air about three feet. When it landed, the whole thing was on fire. Gangsta had already reloaded as he glanced around and saw several niggaz trying to get up off the ground. He also saw T-RU had tossed the street sweeper and pulled out his SP brand Taurus. Gangsta was about to tell him it was time to go, but T-RU ran forward towards the burning truck so Gangsta turned and continued cutting down the drug dealers.

T-RU came around the front of the burning truck and fund Baby Kirk trying to get up off the grass he lay upon. "And I thought you niggaz were some city niggaz," he stated.

Blam! Blam! Blam!
He put three slugs into the center of Baby Kirk's face then gave the area a quick glance and turned to run back to pick up the street sweeper. Both he and Gangsta climbed back into the Hummer. In the distance they could hear the police sirens but Gangsta turned the music up and threw the truck into drive.

Call the cops when you see 2 PAC, grab your Glock's when you see 2 PAC ... Who shot me, but you punks didn't finish now you about to feel the wraith of a menace....

"Please," T-RU smiled. "That nigga been dubbed out."

With the music bumping too loud, they bypassed the police but they seemed to be more concerned about the shooting that had just happen in Kirkwood, they didn't bother with the Hum and its loud music.

* * *

Are you sure you're alright?" Monk asked. He watched as Merrick popped four Tylenol threes into his mouth and began to chew them like they were candy. He wanted to ask if he needed something to drink but when Merrick looked up at him,

Monk saw that both of his eyes were a dark grey color. So, he kept his mouth shut.

"I'm good. It's just as light headache. Y'all ready to do this?" he asked then looked back at Juan, who nodded. He was even more like Monk then he realized because now even he didn't do too much talking. They opened the doors and stepped out.

But Marcellus didn't see three men when he looked out to the parking lot. He watched from a distance as an Italian kid approached, carrying a large army style duffle bag. From the distance he couldn't be sure if it was this kid Donnie or not. Either way it went, he wanted his money. He did have a desire to kill the father too, but for now he would be content with killing this fool.

Marcellus stopped what he was doing and walked out to meet the kid, having never really met him before. None of that mattered, he felt the weight of the .375 under his coat. Both he and the kid stopped nearly ten feet away from one another.

"You Donnie? You bring the money?"

But the kid didn't speak. Marcellus was about to say that this kid was too young. There were often young kids who worked the docks and warehouses, trying to earn an extra dollar or two.

"Yeah, I got your money," Juan said. "You wanna see it?"

Cocky little bastard, Marcellus thought. "Go ahead, show me the money." He almost laughed because it sounded like a cheap commercial line. He watched as the kid unzipped the bag and reached inside, but what he pulled out wasn't money.

"Aw! Fuuuck!" As soon as he saw the S&W model 29. .44 come out of the bag, his hand reached for his own gun but like a Wild West gun battle. He wasn't fast enough and Juan blessed him first.

Booom! Booom!

The .44 spit fire out a foot long as it discharged each slug and Juan's arm jerked slightly. The .44 seem to be his favorite of all the guns Monk had trained him with.

"Hey! What the fuck is going on?" a dock worker shouted.

Marcellus' body was already on the ground. While they were shouting Juan sat the bag down and reached into it again, his bag of toys, he thought. This time he came out with an S and W M and P 15 Semi-automatic rifle.

At the same time both Monk and Merrick stepped from the said of the warehouse. Merrick was defiantly impressed as Juan sprayed the front of the warehouse, taking down at least half of the Irish workers. He made a mental note to be careful with this kid. He was an asset, but could also be a very dangerous enemy. Him and Monk moved into the warehouse and took down everyone inside. The whole thing only took them ten minutes, counting the ones they had to chase to kill.

Soon they were standing over the boxes of counterfeit money, looking at it when Juan pulled the Rang-Rover up to the warehouse and got out.

"What about the money?" Monk asked.

"Its funny money," Merrick told him.

"Yeah, but I could use it to buy guns with," Monk explained. The entire time he was watching Merrick closely.

Merrick glanced at the money, then looked around the warehouse. "You and Juan put the boxes in the Rover, I'm a burn the warehouse so the cops won't find any paraphernalia that suggests they were counterfeiting here. That'll give me time to clean it up for you." Merrick paused almost as if he was listening to something but Monk didn't hear any sirens. "You and Juan can have the money I'm good."

Just before he moved off to start burning the building, Monk noticed that his eyes were now green, with slight tracks of grey in them. He didn't say anything, instead he and Juan started loading the boxes into the truck. By the time they finished Merrick had started the fire and ran back to hop inside the truck.

As they drove away, the flams became larger and brighter in the distance.

Trai'Quan

Chapter Fourteen

"I ain't a killa but don't push me, revenge is like the sweetest joy next to getting pussy. Picture paragraph's unloaded, wise words being quoted, peep the weakness in the rap game explode it."
~2 PAC, Hail Mary.

When Ameed stepped out of the shower and walked into the bedroom, he saw Di'wu lying across the bed naked, watching the 11:00 p.m. news. The speaker was reporting on the shoot out that happened in Kirkwood earlier, but Ameed had already received a call about it. He thought about the 29th law in Robert Greene's book, *Plan all the way to the end*, which was what he had done with this situation.

"So, what's up? You gone watch this gangster shit on TV or are we going to get into some gangster shit?" He watched as she rolled over onto her back and spread her legs. Her pussy was shaved clean and to him it looked like her lips had never been parted, which was such a beautiful sight to his eyes.

"You think you gangster?" She ran a hand from her breast down to part the lips of her pussy, all while looking into his eyes. "Only a true gangster can tame this pussy," she boasted.

Ameed smiled. Thinking, *if only she knew.* "Oh, I've got something for your tough ass." Which really sounded crazy since she only weighed 110 lbs. Ameed climbed onto the bed and stretched out with the towel still wrapped around his waist. He put his head was between her thighs, he knew she liked it when he did this.

Di'wu slid her hand behind his head and guided him to where she wanted him. He slipped his hands under her ass and lifted her towards his face, pushing his tongue out and swiping it across her clit.

Di'wu arched her back and moaned.

Figuring he was in the right spot, he continued to lick as if he were cleaning a plate at the dinner table and then, as his fingers squeezed the twin globes, he pushed his tongue deeper into her and began to fuck her with it.

Di'wu exploded and when she came down, she pulled him up. Soon they were face to face and she was sucking her own juices from his tongue while reaching down between them and guiding him. Di'wu grasp his erection and aimed it at her center. "Now, show me who's gangster." She was breathing heavily.

When she said those words, Ameed smiled because he liked it when she talked tough. He pushed all the way into her deeply, on the first thrust. Taking her breath as he did.

Di'wu raised her hips up off the bed to meet him and Ameed grasp her ass with one hand, still using the other to balance himself. He held her in a raised position while he pistoled in and out of her, starting with slow strokes and then speeding up. She locked her legs around his waist and her arms around his neck as she held on.

Just when Ameed felt himself about to spill his seed inside of her, he remembered that they weren't wearing a condom.

* * *

"Are you sure about this?" The guy asked.

"Nigga, don't it look like I'm sure?" Cutt looked over into Miles' face, they were both sitting inside of his truck. "This nigga killed yo man, Shawty. Shawty, I'm willing to pay you just to get even. But listen, Shawty, if you ain't built like that, then I can always find somebody else who wants to make a little change."

Miles looked over at Cutt as he sat behind the wheel. Something inside of his being kept telling him that this nigga wasn't right, but he had heard the rumors in the streets that Lee-Lee had taken a contract on this nigga Judah and missed. When the news came that Lee-Lee had been murdered, the first thing that was being said was that Judah got him.

"Nigga, I can handle whatever," Miles told him. "Don't no nigga question my gun play. How much you putting up anyway?"

"Sheeeiit, Shawty." Cutt leaned back on the door and looked at him. "I wasn't gone put but a stack and a half on it. I mean, it's all I got right now, Shawty, you want that or not?"

Miles was sure he'd given Lee-Lee at least two grand for the hit. Everybody knew that Judah wasn't below keeping $1500 all to himself. That was a nice check, too, seeing as he was going after that nigga Judah, anyway. Might as well get some free bread with it.

"Where it at, Shawty?"

Cutt pulled the money out of his dash board.

Miles saw that there was more money in there and what looked like some crack. For a minute he thought about just taking this niggas money and robbing him, but he pushed the thought aside. First, he needed to see about this nigga Judah, then he'd take care of Cutt's slimy ass. Sheeeiit, free money was good money to him.

The deal was going down in the parking lot of the old Regency Square Mall, which had gone out of business due to the fact that the land it was built on wasn't stable. The mall had begun to sink and the people who owned it didn't know what to do with the land. Now it was just an abandoned building and a large parking lot that had sink holes in it.

Ant-G swung the dark blue Cutlass over to the curb and watched as his partner, Reon, looked over the parking lot carefully.

"Time to make this money, thug," Ant-G stated.

But Reon didn't speak, instead he sat quietly as Ant-G pulled the car around to what used to be the back of the mall. At the moment, there wasn't anyone out there but them.

"What's up, thug? Where this nigga at?" Reon asked.

This was supposed to be a simple deal. The way Ant-G had explained it, he'd been trying to find someone that he could buy some major weight from. With all of the real die-hard dope boys from the bottom just up and leaving, they were about to take their hustle down there but they needed some serious work. Then just a couple of days ago, Ant-G got word from Cat-eye that a nigga he knew could drop it on them. Ant-G had called the number Cat-eye gave him and set up this deal.

"Just hold tight, thug," Ant-G told him. He checked the time on his Kenneth Cole watch. "We like ten minutes early. This nigga said he was gone come through at 11:00."

Ant-G was thinking about how sweet this deal was. This nigga was about to see him a brick for $16,500. Wasn't no other nigga in Augusta dishing out work like that. When the nigga Cat-eye pulled up and they bumped heads at the Citgo, Ant-G thought that it was too good to be true. The nigga said he'd moved his whole operation to Atlanta, said the nigga Ameed had put him on to some real nice shit. So, when Ant-G told him that he was looking for his own come up, Cat-eye suggested he call this nigga that he knew. Ant-G made the call and it just so happened the nigga said he had one brick left. When he asked Ant-G what he had, all he had was 14,000, but the dude said that he couldn't do it for less than 16,500.

That's when Ant-G pulled Reon into the play and together they came up with the sixteen-five. *Damn*, Ant-G was thinking.

He wondered what kind of hook up the nigga Ameed put Cat-eye up on. Shit, he'd always thought that nigga was a lame, always hanging with that busts his sister used to go with.

It was just as he saw the head lights of the cocaine white Mercedes, AMG coupe turning into the parking lot, that he thought, "*I wonder if the Cops ever got that sucka ass nigga.*"

"Come on, that's gotta be my guy," he told Reon.

Before he exited the car, Reon lifted his shirt and pushed his mama's .357 down into the front of his Roca-wear jeans. Ant-G grabbed the bag with the loot in it as the AMG stopped a little over ten feet away from them, but kept its headlights on.

They watched as the driver's side door opened and a tall guy stepped out of the coupe. The guy was wearing a two thousand dollar double breasted, cream colored, wool suit that seem to be tailored. He also wore a calf length, white wool, trench coat that seem to immediately start flapping in the wind as he exited the car. It was because of the white and beige fedora the man wore that they couldn't see his facial features, but they did see that he held a 12-inch square shaped looking object in his hand.

"Uhm, you Mr. Black, right? I'm Ant-G and I've got the whole sixteen-five right here." While he was talking, Ant-G looked over at Reon with a smile that said *I told you nigga.*

For some reason, Reon had been watching this nigga in the white suit and he suddenly realized that what the nigga held in his hand was a McDonald's bag. He got a real bad feeling in his gut.

"Ayo, GD, folk," Reon mumbled. "Something ain't right."

"What?" Ant-G said, but it was at this time that everything seem to go horribly wrong.

The MacDonald's bag dropped and it seemed like it was falling in slow motion. Ant-G had just looked that way after Reon finished speaking and saw the guy reach under his trench coat and swing out the pistol grip, Nicole plated 12-gauge pump.

"Oh, shiiiit! It's a hiiit!" Ant-G screamed.

The man squeezed the trigger just as Ant-G turned to flee.

Kah-boom!

Fire spit from the barrel at least a foot long. The first slug tore into Ant-G's torsos and ripped his flesh away as if it really wasn't attached to his body to begin with.

Kah-chink!

He cocked the shotgun, sending another shell into the chamber.

Ant-G was still turning, trying to land on the side of the car, away from the shotgun.

Kah-boom!

Somehow Reon managed to get the .357 out as he spun to his side. His mistake, however, was that he'd seen too many gangster movies and he tried to hold the large pistol sideways and shoot.

Bam! Bam! Bam!

Every shot went wild, the .357 was just too powerful to be shot that way. The shots went higher or wider as his arm jerked. He saw the second shotgun slug throw Ant-G up onto the hood of the Cutlass and yelled, "Shit!"

Ka-chink!

Reon was just about to duck down on the passenger side of the car when he heard the sound and looked back one last time to aim the .357 for another shot.

Kaboom!

The last time the pump spoke the slug nearly took Reon's head off his shoulders and then everything went silent.

Mr. Black stood there for a minute. Holding the shotgun in his hands, listening. After he was sure the two men were dead, he bent down and picked up the bag he'd dropped. He walked towards the car and then stood over Ant-G's body. He opened the bag and turned it upside down, emptying what was inside, onto the body.

Out of the bag fell a dead rat and several pieces of yellow cheese, all of which landed on Ant-G's body.

"That's how I feel about rats," Mr. Black said and spit on the body.

He turned to walk back to the AMG when Detective Bradley mentioned that Ant-G was the one who told him about who he hung with and that was how he tracked him to Atlanta. He'd told himself that the young nigga was a peon and wasn't worth the trouble, but that part of him which was Mr. Black simply couldn't see letting this known snitch live. If only they knew how he felt about rodents and why.

That thought about his past was what he left the scene with.

Chapter Fifteen

Milan Giovanni and his wife Julia were really finding it hard to believe. Here they were, not only inside of the States with legal papers and Documents, but the house was simply amazing. It was located just off I-985, right before reaching Lake Lanier, in a nice gated community. It was a two-story home with 4 bedrooms, 3 1/2 baths, a large kitchen, living room and dining room, along with a large den. Every room boasted the finest furniture and exquisite art. The house had an extensive backyard with a carport to the side. Parked in the driveway were the Mercedes 500 SL and the Infiniti Q 35, both were silver in color. In all, the house and both cars were a small fortune themselves. This was all made possible by their future son-in-law.

Of their family, their three girls and two of their sons came with them. That didn't include Ann and Juan, but Anna had a house that was located not very far from theirs. Their other three sons were left behind in Italy and were now in control of the winery, which was being rebuilt, also a gift from Merrick.

Together with Don Sirrelli, Merrick added onto the dowry considerably. In fact, it was now even more than what was initially promised and on the business aspect, Merrick was only asking for 15% commission. The winery was now about to become a major business. Merrick somehow had been able to make a deal with the people who produced Merlot champagnes and they'd sent some of their people out to show Milan's sons how to establish a winery that met their standards.

However, the most important gift was to come from the older Don. Mr. Sirrelli had gone before the Sicilian Mafia's board and petitioned for Milan to receive a Donship. With the upgrade to the winery and the alcohol store that Merrick legally established in his name in the States, Milan was made an official Under Boss. To fully become a Don, he had yet to undergo the trial and error of the families here with in the States, but he knew that he was ready to face it.

Milan sighed. All of this was made possible because of his daughter and the marriage that would take place in the upcoming weeks.

* * *

The Oshein family was represented in New York City by two brothers, both of them pure blooded Irish men from the old country, Robert, or rather Bobby Oshein and Jacob Oshein. Most people assumed that the Irish mafia was a very large structure and powerful. However, they did have some numbers but their physical power also came from an alliance they shared with the Russian Mafiosi. That business alliance was built upon the two factions coming together to create money. Literally, counterfeit money.

But the Russian's were never one's to be seen in the spot light, they kept a distance and played the shadows. That was until now, with the death of the Irish's designated Boss and the loss of the money they'd been waiting on, it became inevitable that the Russian's would come forward.

"God! I really hate this bitch," Jacob Oshein stated.

At 5 '11" with his pale skin and reddish blond hair color, he was the perfect image of an Irishman. Unlike his brother, whose hair was oily black and his height was unmistakable at 6'4" with a gangly build. Jacob was the younger of the two, being thirty-eight and the most reckless, while Bobby, at forty-one, was more sensible and mentally stable.

Bobby sat on the hood of their Audi A-8, while Jacob stood next to him. The bitch whom he was referring to had just pulled up in a Lexus LS coupe, which was followed by a black on black Land-Rover. All of them were currently parked inside of the warehouse parking lot, down on the Brooklyn docks. But not the same warehouse were their men died not long ago.

Bobby watched as the *bitch* exited the coupe wearing a $3000 Ferragano, designer dress and $1700 Giuseppe Zanetti 3 1/2-inch stiletto heels. The heels only boosted her original 6 '1 frame, showing off her extremely long, elegant legs. The tall Russian woman also had long blond hair and thick lips that looked as if they had been stung by a bee. Bobby and Jacob also noticed the four very large, Russian men who looked like they were body builders who exited the truck and followed closely behind her. The way they looked around said that they took their jobs seriously.

"Gentlemen," the woman tilted her head in acknowledgement.

"Claudia," Bobby nodded.

"Zo', who's going to be the one to explain what happened to me?" she asked.

Claudia Oleg Valimir was called *The Voice*. She wasn't the head of the Russian Mafiosi, they wouldn't place a woman in such a powerful position. Instead, she was like a secretary.

Bobby sighed then explained what they knew, which was that no Italians were found dead at the warehouse and the money wasn't recovered. Nor were there any witnesses.

"Zo'," Claudia Oleg Valimir began. "Iz dez Italians who violated ze business agreement? Dis iz what you are telling me?"

Both of the Irishmen hunched their shoulders as she looked closely at each one of them, almost as if she was a human lie detector. Her gaze was extremely penetrating and intimidating.

"Alright, zo, who waz diz agreement with?"

"A Mob Captain named Niccolo' Carmen that lives over in lower Manhattan. He has a house on Grand street," Bobby stated. "Guy has some type of furniture store over in Washington Heights," he added. He waited while it seemed she was processing the information she'd just received.

As the Secretary, Claudia was the representative of Dimitri Svetlovi, who in turn was the head of the Russian criminal organization. Not many people saw Dimitri in the flesh, instead they were visited by his 'voice' and she seemed to be empowered by him directly.

"Zo you think dis mob captain iz playing gamez?"

"Maybe," Bobby replied. "Look, we're going to take care of it."

"And ze money?"

"If we can't get it back from these guys," Bobby explained. "Then we'll have to make up for it. You know we still have that gold job coming up. We'll work something out on that deal."

They watched as she nodded her head then without further word, she turned and walked back to her car. The muscle also returned to their Land-Rover and both vehicles left.

As soon as they were out of sight, Jacob turned and looked at Bobby. "The fuck? Are you stupid? We are *not* taking the short end of the stick on this gold job!"

They were now leaving the warehouse district with Bobby driving. "Oh, yeah? You do realize that we can't pull this off without their people, right? And we don't need any bad blood between us, especially right about now."

Jacob twisted his face up but turned his head to look out the window.

"Look, don't worry about it. We'll settle this suit with Niccolo' and that'll be the end of it."

"I'm really not taking any shorts on this gold deal Bobby!" Jacob stated, but Bobby remained silent.

This entire gold job came to them out of the blue. Twice a year, the Federal Reserve Bank in New York would swap out

gold bars with the Swiss Banks. The reason being, in Switzer-
land, it was common for the banks to come into possession of
certain gold bricks. Which were from either Hitler or Stalin's
time, or simply from a time where a lot of items were stolen
from Russia. Most of this gold was reddish yellow, which
meant it held some copper impurities, suggesting that the bars
were re-casted, melted down coins, jewelry or even statues.

The Federal Reserve Bank in New York would swap some
of its pure bright butter yellow, almost 100% pure gold, for
some of this reddish gold. A trade that amounted to every bul-
lion of reddish yellow gold being equal only to 1/4 that of the
pure butter yellow gold. So, for every one of the butter yellow
gold bullions, the Swiss would trade four of their mixed reddish
yellow bullions. A trade that only happened two times a year.

Somehow the Russian's found out about the delivery and
agreed to split the take with them if they were willing to help
on the heist. It was estimated to be something like forty or fifty
million, per shipment. So, Bobby understood why Jacob didn't
want to take that loss.

* * *

"Are you ready for the big day?"
Merrick glanced over to where Ameed sat across from him
inside of the stretched Lincoln Navigator. There were five of
them inside of the limo, he, Ameed, Monk and Juan as well as
Ameed's new street partner, Judah. Since he'd given Ameed the
green light to indulge in street issues, Ameed had taken a page
from his play book. The part where whatever side dealings they
did didn't come back to harm the company that they'd founded.
Thus, Ameed had designated Judah to be his hands-on person
to deal with both T-RU and Cat-eye. What that really meant was

that Judah was responsible for getting the cocaine for them from Di'wu and her people in little China.

"I'm not even sure yet," Merrick responded.

"Bruh, there's no such thing as you're not sure. This is your life we're talking about here," Ameed explained as he leaned over and poured some more Pinot Noir into everyone's glass, since he was the one holding the bottle. "Marriage is a life time commitment, bruh. A man and his woman entering into a partnership of unbreakable matrimony. I'm not talking about in the same way that people who don't mean it do it. Son...,"

"I think that I get the picture, bruh," Merrick said as he sipped his champagne. "I'm not having doubts about the actual event. It's just...," he faltered. Falling into his thoughts and at the same time not noticing that both Monk and Juan were looking at him funny. Merrick was thinking about his mental imbalance. He was worried that he wouldn't be able to keep his dealings from his family and then there was the possibility of him passing something off to his kids.

"It's just what, bruh?" Ameed asked then watched as Merrick shook his head.

"I'm just trying to imagine being married with all of the extra stuff going on. That's all."

"Sun, listen," Ameed started. "I know you're a smart guy. I've been rocking with you long enough to know. I'm sure you already know how you need to set it up but yo, you know what the smartest thing you did was?"

The question left Merrick vexed. "Nah. What's that?"

"You didn't make one of these hood chicks a wife. No offense to Kenya, may she rest in peace," Ameed said. "What you did when you went and found Anna, bruh, she's Italian. She was born and bred with certain codes of loyalty inside of her. The stuff runs in their blood, I mean look at your brother in law there." He nodded to Juan, who sat next to Merrick sipping his own glass of champagne.

Merrick looked over and as usual, Juan didn't show any emotion.

"Que' unda?" Juan asked in Spanish. "What's up?'

Merrick knew that Ameed didn't know the half of it about Juan and he wasn't about to tell him. Instead he smiled at the boy and started to understand exactly what Ameed was trying to explain to him.

* * *

At that exact moment, in an Escalade stretch limo, Jennifer, her Mom Tiffany, Anna and her mom Julia, were also sipping champagne.

"So, are you about ready to officially become my sister in law?" Jen asked.

She and Anna were seated on the same side, talking while both of their mother's did the same on their side of the limo.

Anna smiled. "I already feel like we're sisters."

"I know, right? But we'll be able to spend more time together." Jen sipped her drink. "I have few true friends as it is and I know Snipes, you two wouldn't be getting married if he didn't feel like you were the right woman for him."

"Really?" Anna asked. She wasn't really surprise to hear it. She and Merrick spent a lot of time together when he was around. "Do you think he'll want a large family?"

Although he had told her that he would. She wasn't sure if he was serious or not, while she was.

"Girl, please. Snipes has already given you that big ass house. I know y'all gone fill it with little ones." Jen laughed. She was referring to the house that Anna was already living in.

Since Merrick wasn't going to violate the rules, he wasn't sleeping there with her. Instead, Jen was living with her until the wedding.

"The way I see it, all you've gotta do is maintain your figure after the babies" Jen said.

"With all of the shopping and running around we do," Anna said, "I don't see how I'll keep any weight on."

Merrick had set up a joint bank account for him and her and made sure that she had all of the necessary credit cards for shopping. At one point, she'd thought that she was spending too much of his money, but after he sat her down and explained that she was supposed to spend the money, she felt more comfortable about it. Now it seemed she and Jen went shopping every weekend.

"Shoot, that ain't the half of it." Jen laughed. "Now that he bought that jet, we can go shopping all over the world."

Merrick had recently purchased a used, Citation Sovereign, mid-sized, business jet, which had a lot of space and held up to eight passengers. That didn't include the pilot's and the two flight attendants.

"Yeah, he did say that we could use it if they weren't using it for business," Anna laughed, too.

They'd already used the jet when they flew to Paris, where she had her wedding dress made. Anna knew what Merrick was and she had no problem with it. Her only aim was to make and keep him happy.

All of her life, she'd dreamed about this type of life style. She read about it in books, seen it on TV and in movies and now she was about to live it. Anna fully intended to be loyal and devoted to Merrick in every way imaginable because in truth, *he* was now *her* life partner and this life was all too real.

Chapter Sixteen

The club that they took Merrick to was in Las Vegas. They'd taken the Cattani, which was the name he had painted on the side of the white jet. When Merrick first decided to buy the jet, after being allowed to use Don Sirrelli's, he'd explained that its official use was for him and Ameed in terms of business. But when there weren't any business plans made at least a week in advance, it could be used by only a hand full of other people, besides them.

At the moment, that was neither here nor there, he knew that this whole weekend was his bachelor's party. Anna was having her own thing with his sister and both their mothers, who had driven down to Miami for the weekend in one of the limos.

The club they were going to in Vegas was called Three-E'S, which stood for Exotic, Envy and Ecstasy. It was located at Mandalay Bay, which was on Las Vegas Blvd. S. It was originally built to be a part of the MGM Resorts International, but some rich guy bought it and converted it into one of the hottest night clubs in Vegas.

The inside wasn't like anything that Merrick had ever seen before and that was also, in part, due to that fact that he didn't make it a habit to attend clubs. Here, there was a lot of expensively dressed, mixed people, be they black, white, or even Hispanic, present. The dance floor was huge and there was a stage and two bars, one down on the center floor and one up in the Terrance, which actually held the VIP sky boxes.

Ameed, being the leader of this expedition, led them to the entrance of the VIP section. Once there, he moved forward to speak with the blond-haired girl who was accepting the money.

"Hello, beautiful." He smiled at the woman.

"Hi, how may I help you?" She asked.

"Well, seeing as we're having a bachelor's party this week-end, my guy here is about to get married next week, me and the fellas wanna see if we can find our way into the VIP section. What we need to know is, just how hard it'll be for us to do that."

"Oh, gee. Those boxes are reserved. They have to be asked for at least a day in advance," she explained.

"I see. So, what you're basically telling me is...," Ameed took his time at this point. He dug into his pocket and withdrew a nice wad of bills that were secured by a gold money clip, which had diamond studs on it. They all watched as the girls' eyes also took in the bills.

Ameed glanced around like he was a crook about to rob the place. "You don't have *any* boxes that aren't currently in use, at this moment?" he asked rhetorically.

"Uh maybe." They girl also glanced around. She watched as Ameed peeled off two thousand dollars and very discreetly slid them to her. The girl, who couldn't have been any older than twenty-five, looked around and then slid the money into her pocket.

"Ah, here it is, Mr. Chase. You're in sky box eight, which also comes with the complementary two bottles of Chablis. Hold on just a minute, I'll have someone show you and your lady to the box," she stated professionally.

* * *

"What club?" Anna asked as she followed close behind Jen. Both Tiffany and Julia were in front of them.

"It's a male strip club," Jen explained. "It's where women go to watch men take their clothes of while they dance. You've never heard of one?"

"I've heard about men going to watch women do that, but I never knew that women could watch men do it," Anna replied.

With it being an upscale club, they let Tiffany do the talking and she bribed the guy at the door. Neither Jen nor Anna were twenty years old yet. Nevertheless, they made it in and even ended up with a VIP section.

"Do you think Merrick will be mad if he found out we came here?" Anna asked as they seated themselves.

There were men dancing throughout the club, up on mini stages that were close to either the tables or the entire VIP area.

"Girl, listen,"Jen started.

Tiffany asked for a bottle of Riesling to be brought on ice. The champagne cost nearly a thousand dollars a bottle.

"I know Snipes," Jen continued. "He's not going to be mad at you for looking. As long as you don't let any of these guys look at your stuff naked, touch your stuff, or get inside of your stuff, he isn't going to be mad. Think of this as sex education 101."

The champagne arrived and Tiffany poured for everyone as a half-naked man started dancing up on the mini stage before them. Both Jen and Anna bobbed their heads to the music, while Tiffany and Julia squealed with laughter. Anna knew that, like her, her mother had never experienced anything like this before.

As she watched, she saw that her mother was having fun. She thought about the fact that her mother and father had been together a little over twenty-nine years and if her mother could have fun like this and it didn't bother her, then she wouldn't worry too much about it. Then she imagined that Merrick was also at one of these clubs somewhere, having fun and only *looking*, she hoped.

* * *

Merrick was too high. They'd just finished smoking a third blunt since entering the club.

"Ayo, listen, sun, I'm telling you," Ameed was in the process of saying in Merrick's ear. "What we need to do is get some of these city officials and politicians into our pocket. Me in Atlanta and since you've got the expansion going on up in Atlantic City, shit, we could get some judges, lawyers and even a few of the DA's on our team. Make some donations to charity and even help out at some of the children's hospitals. Once we put it down like that, shit the FBI, IRS or whoever, those fools won't even look our way."

While he spoke, Merrick was wondering who had revealed his plan. Everything Ameed said was actually a part of what Merrick was trying to build and he'd already taken some steps with Sirrelli. Plus, he'd just acquired another casino that had also been just as low budget as the Cattani once was.

Andretti ended up being the biggest idiot ever, having sold his shares of the casino to Borges, who Sirrelli had convinced to make the offer, using Merrick's money. Merrick, in turn, also paid him for the favor. In the end, Borges also happened to have another casino that he was willing to part with, The Starlight, which Merrick purchased whole and was now undergoing its own remodeling. He had Berry over seeing that as well.

He'd found the perfect Pit Boss to govern both casinos, thanks to Agent Simkins. His sister Jackie was an asset. Merrick had her and her son relocated to Atlantic City and he upgraded their life style. He'd set up a college fund for her son so he could pretty much go and become anything that he wanted to be, as part of the unspoken agreement between him and Agent Simkins.

* * *

Judah was also listening. Having gone through everything he had, he still didn't know who put the hits on him. But there was a rumor in the streets, one he'd heard just a few days ago. It seemed this crack head ass nigga, Miles, was putting the word out that he was looking for him. The only reason he hadn't stepped to the fool yet was because of Ameed. Ameed pretty much told him that the reason he was with them this weekend was because of the position he now held as his right hand or street enforcer. Part of which, Judah knew. It meant that he had to think every situation through and where there was conflict, he had to handle it without it coming back on the company. On top of all that, Ameed was currently in the process of converting an old bar he bought into a studio, which Judah would also be running.

He'd already pulled Phat aside, he wanted Phat to be there first artist off M and A Musiq. Those were his exact thoughts, he would get Phat to do a nice CD and Ameed said he had some connections in New York, said he knew somebody that DJ at Hot 97. That meant if he could get a few hot tracks to jump up North then he could get Phat into some major shit.

But even as he thought about all of this, Judah still knew that he was going to have to find out who it was that was trying to have him touched.

Niccolo' Carmen, or rather Nicky, wasn't a real big Italian guy. He was of average size and stood at 5'10", with black hair with hard eyes. There was a scar that started just over his right eye and slanted down over his nose, which stopped half way down his cheek. The scar came from a car accident he'd been in when he was younger.

As he walked up the street, Nicky took the time to speak to some of the neighborhood kids. He even dug into his pocket and pulled out a few coins, which he gave them then continued on his way. He had to duck inside an alley as a short cut to where he was going and was half way through the alley when the late model Ford Taurus pulled in and sped up. He was turning and about to hop out of the way but the car suddenly stopped close to him. Four Irish thugs jumped out, two of them he knew already.

"Bobby, I've been meaning to get into contact with ya," Nicky said.

"Is that right, Nicky? What were you going to do? Give us our freakin money back?" Bobby asked.

That's when Nicky noticed that the two other guys standing behind Bobby and his brother were holding baseball bats in their hands.

"Hey. Look here, guys," Nicky tried to speak.

"No, you look here, Nicky. We've got too many dead Irish and a lot of missing money but no freakin' answers. So, here's what we're going to do, we're going to break every freakin' bone in your body until you tell us where our shit is. Do you hear that you freakin shmuck?" Bobby asked and then he gave the word.

The two thugs with the bats came forward and commenced to beating Nicky with them. The beating was a good long one too and when Bobby realized that Nicky wasn't going to talk, he put a stop to it.

"Alright, Nicky, here's the deal. I know how you Italians are but right about now we're not even worried about a vendetta, we just want our freakin' money back. You've got three days to come up with the money, or we sack you and everybody standing close to you." Bobby squatted down right where Nicky's head was as he explained the situation to him. "Do you understand what I'm trying to tell you Nicky? The next time we won't be this nice about it."

When he stood up and looked down, Bobby saw that Nicky was coughing up blood.

* * *

The ringing of the phone woke Charlie up out of his much-needed sleep, which he'd been really enjoying. He had been spending a lot of time at his restaurant lately and had lost a lot of sleep. When the bed side phone came alive in the middle of the night, he reluctantly rolled over and reached for it.

"Hello?" His voice sounding like it was more tired than he was.

"We've got a situation with these Irish," the voice said.

Charlie wiped the sleep from his face with his free hand and glanced behind him, seeing that his wife was still asleep. "Run it by me."

He listened as the caller explained to him what had happened to Nicky. He already knew the part about the Irish being killed at the warehouse, he also knew about Peralli's son stealing the counterfeit money, which set all of this into motion. He knew, because he was actually the one to suggest that Donnie steal the money and bring it to him. What he didn't know was how Peralli' killed every Irish that was at that warehouse and he hadn't asked.

But now Charlie knew the thing had gone bad and something had to be done to avoid a war between the Italians and the Irish mafia. Charlie sighed. "Okay. I'll take care of it. Make sure Nicky's alright. Put somebody in the hallway outside his room," he instructed and then ended the call. Charlie fell backwards facing the ceiling. What the fuck could he do?

* * *

Paul Peralli' also received a call that night, telling him the same thing. His call was more of a warning. They were warning any and everybody that had some type of dealings with the Irish. However, the caller didn't know just how deep Paul's dealings went, so when the caller ended the call, Paul fumbled to find his eye glasses. He managed to dial another number then looked at the clock and saw that it was late.

"Yeah! The Irish jumped Nicky Carmen," Paul said. "They're saying they want their money in three days."

"They know about Donnie?"

"I'm not sure," Paul stated. "Look, Don Sirrelli, I don't know what to do. I'm scared for myself and my family. It seems like this problem just won't go away."

"Relax," Sirrelli said. "They say three days huh? Well, don't worry about it. Get some sleep Paul, it's still late."

The phone call ended and Paul replaced the receiver back on the base. He was wondering if the problem was even possible to solve.

* * *

"Shit!" Merrick rolled over and reached for his cell phone. He glanced at the time before he answered and saw that it was 7:30 a.m. "Yeah. Who's this?"

"It's me." The voice said.

He immediately knew who *me* was. "A'ight,"

"That thing you did for me. About those comic books? Well the problem came back."

Merrick caught on that the call was about the Irish. Something else must've happened. "You know there's only one way to really solve the problem. I've told you that already," Merrick said. He heard the other person sigh.

"When's the wedding?"

"In eleven days," he replied.

"Can you do this in three for me? And after that I don't wanna hear anything else about it," the voice said.

"Depends on how you want me to solve it," Merrick answered.

There was a pause.

"I'm sick of hearing about it. So, use your best judgement, I trust you in these types of situations."

The call ended and Merrick looked at the phone and thought out loud, "His best judgement?" At that moment, if he could have looked into a mirror, he'd have seen the grey in his eyes shift, becoming the dominant shade.

Trai'Quan

153

Chapter Seventeen

Merrick debated seriously on whether he should have brought Monk and Juan with him, but he didn't honestly see why he would need them. Plus, he was really starting to think that he was having a nervous breakdown or something.

He sat in the E-320 sedan and watched as the two Irish men ate and drank coffee inside the diner. It hadn't been hard to find them, there wasn't very many places for them to be and no one even questioned why a black man was asking about the Irish. It was evident that there was something going on between the Irish and the Italians.

Merrick's attention was drawn to the LS Coupe that pulled into the parking lot, followed closely by the Land Rover. He didn't know what pulled his attention to them but he watched as the tall woman exited the Lexus and the four tough guys got out of the truck. All five of them entered the diner, but only the woman sat the table with the Irish, the four tough guys sat in a booth next to them.

Something made Merrick write down the tag numbers of both vehicles, he wasn't sure if they were Irish or not but better to be safe than stupid. He would have someone look into them when he got the chance, but for now he continued to sit there and watch. The whole thing looked like some type of meeting, yet he couldn't be 100% sure either way.

Inside the diner, they discussed the plan.

"We're going to have to make a deal," Bobby said.

Beside him he could feel the heat coming off his brother, but they had discussed it already. They honestly didn't think that Nicky would come up with the money and the more time that went by, they knew there was a greater possibly that he would bring more Italians in to it. Also, they now had another name, someone remembered something about a kid named

Donnie who was working at the warehouse and since they knew the only bodies found were Irish, they now suspected this kid might have had something to do with it.

"Iz good," Claudia said. "De job will be in zix weekz. We will make de deal, then."

It seemed like that concluded the meeting. They watched as she stood and turned to leave with the three stooges following.

Merrick was still watching and debating on whether he should follow the Lexus and Land Rover or not. Nobody had told him about these people. He just had a feeling that this woman was important somehow. Instead, he pulled out his new Blackberry and text the information of the plates to someone along with a brief message. Just as he finished, the two Irish brothers came out of the diner.

* * *

"Where the fuck is this bitch?" The guy exclaimed as he sat back on the sofa. He had been trying to get in her panties all day, actually for the last couple of days and he really didn't like hanging around her parents' house like this. She said they had gone to the matinee and would be gone for at least three hours. He was just trying to do his thing and leave.

Ever since he showed up in Little Italy with pockets full of money, girls were throwing themselves at him left and right, but this girl Barbara, he really wanted to get down with her. She was one of those stuck up types, thought that she was all of that. So, when he turned the juice up and she told him to come over, he knew that this was it. Not to mention he was running low on cash too.

At the moment, the girl was upstairs in her bedroom doing something. She'd said that she would be back in a second but that was five minutes ago. Then he heard the footsteps on the stairs.

"Finally. It's about time," he began saying.

The stairs were behind the sofa where he sat, so he wasn't looking at her as he spoke.

"I thought you were going to wait until, oh, fuck! Oh, shit!"

When Donnie turned his head, he found himself looking into the eyes of the well-dressed black man. He was aware of the .22 in the guy's hands, with the sound suppressor attached to the end of it, but there was nothing that Donnie could do.

"Oh God! Man, please don't kill me. Jesus, please," he begged.

Instead of saying anything, the guy stood there silently, like a serial killer. Then he squeezed the trigger, placing two parabellums into his chest and one into his forehead.

As he turned to leave, Mr. Black gave a brief thought to the dead girl upstairs, not that he cared. He exited the house by the back door. Jumped the fence that enclosed the yard and made it back to the E-320, where he pulled out a bottle of Tylenol threes. He got into the car and started, then turned and began to leave Brooklyn.

While driving he reached into his coat and withdrew the business card. Merrick looked at it, Dr. Jean von Raleigh, psychiatric/psychologist. East Orange N.J. He'd already made an appointment for the next day. He was convinced that he really had a serious problem. Too many times over the last three months he'd found himself doing things that he didn't understand, or dreamed about things that didn't make much sense to him. Especially those dreams where he called himself Mr. Black. That didn't make any sense to him at all.

Earlier today, when he'd killed Paul Peralli', his wife and baby girl, Merrick knew then that something wasn't right. He would never have thought that he could stand over a baby's crib and do what he'd done. Some part of him had been able to and that bothered him. Even the headaches were worse.

* * *

This nigga couldn't have made it this easy Judah was thinking when he saw the F-150 at the Texaco on Glenwood Rd, not too far from Line St, which was also where he'd caught that nigga Lee-Lee. He wasn't even looking for this nigga Miles when he saw him.

"You better ride wit ya fire or stay ya ass home, why you in a muthafuckin choppa zone. All day niggaz ridin round wit day chrome...."

"Yeah," he answered, ending the ring tone.

"Somebody was just over here asking about Lee-Lee."

Judah knew who the caller was because she was the one to tell him where he could find Lee-Lee in the first place. "Oh yeah? What you tell 'em?"

Watching as Miles stood at the gas pump next to his truck, talking to some female that was driving a Skyline, the crackhead said, "Humpf. Nothing. I ain't no rat."

Oh yeah, he thought. "What the nigga driving?"

She described the blue truck as Judah pulled into the parking lot of the bowling alley. He turned his smoke grey, 2010 Camaro so that he could still see Miles, but he didn't turn the car off, he kept it running.

"Look," he said into the phone. "I appreciated the heads up. I'm a swing through in a few, I've got a little something for you." He ended the call just as he watched the girl put her number into Miles' phone. "I wonder if she knows this nigga is gay," he said to no one.

Not only was Atlanta quickly becoming the major city for gay rights, but word was, when Miles was at Macon State

157

Prison, he had a thing for sneaking around with the homosexuals. *Nasty dick nigga*, he thought. It wasn't surprising. Rumor was, he'd become a Muslim but once he hit the streets, he was smoking crack and eating pork again, like the shit was going out of style.

Judah laughed as he watched Miles hop back into his truck. He remembered one time over hearing the nigga *As-salaam Alaikum* a nigga about three months ago. He bent forward and reached under the passenger seat, pulling out the Beretta 9mm and checking the clip.

"Might as well, I ain't got nothing else to do right now."

Miles had no idea he was being watched. He couldn't stop cheesing as he put the truck into drive and pulled out of the gas station. The little bitch he just met was visiting some of her family. She was originally from Ft. Lauderdale Florida but came to Atlanta for a funeral.

He turned, then drove past the golf course. He was smiling because the bitch said that they could hook up later and she was too fine. He turned onto Hooper Street and slowed the truck. He was looking for this nigga who always wore the Falcons starter jacket. The nigga usually had some good deals on the dope and he was trying to get his smoke on. Miles had already been smoking ice for the past three days and hadn't been to sleep since. He still hadn't found that nigga Judah either. Nevertheless, the word was out, he defiantly wasn't hiding.

Then he saw the all-white starter jacket with the large Atlanta Falcon on it, out lined in red. Miles stuck his arm out the window as he stopped the truck. Then waved at the nigga. "Ayo! Shawty!"

The dope boy looked up and Miles saw him smile. *Pussy ass nigga. Think it's funny to get my money. If we was the in prison I'd get that niggas money.* Those were his thoughts as he waited while the dope boy walked in the direction of his truck.

On the radio, a Lil Boosie song was just coming on so he began to bob his head and sing along.

You ain't bout what you be talkin' bout, uh...uh...You ain't ready for yo people to be walk-in out, uh...uh...

Miles had been caught up in singing so he wasn't paying attention to his surroundings. Some of it was because of his lack of sleep. When he saw movement out of his peripheral vision, he assumed that it was the dope boy, having finally reached the truck, but that was the last assumption he ever made.

Bam! Bam! Bam! Bam!

All of the dope boys standing around watched as the figure wearing the black fitted hat strolled up to the truck's driver side and pushed the gun through the window, easily delivering the four even shots.

"Oh shiiit, Shawty...! You see that?"

"Damn, Shawty! Who that gangsta is?"

"I dunno, Shawty, probably that nigga."

Judah tuned the voices out as he glanced around. He didn't see any Cops so he tucked his head, hoping none of these Neighborhood Watch niggaz saw his face. Then he walked off as if nothing had happened. He had parked the Camaro further up the street, but he knew he was going to have to replace it.

The overall structure of the Cartel is usually built upon six principals and it has several individual family bodies. Ameed was thinking about this structure as he sat in his office and studied the information on his computer. The political government, or conducting of said government, shall be related to, or concerned with, making a distinguished administration of government policy. The six principal's which construct such an entity are:

1. The Cabinet
2. The Acquaintance
3. The Racket
4. The Tactical
5. The Elevation
6. The Loyalist

What he was reading was a piece he'd found on the internet and it was said that the piece was posted by someone who had real South American ties. Ameed didn't know how true that was, but he was researching because Snipes had given him complete power over this end of the business. That meant that *everything* that happened in Georgia and any new area that he established business in, was all his call. All Snipes had to say was that Ameed was responsible and had to handle it with a professional mannerism.

1. The Cabinet- is equal to being - A body of advisers of a head of state (As a sovereign or President). A similar advisory council of a governor of a state or Mayor.

What he thought that meant was that the council which governs whatever the activity, is responsible for each individual's area of expertise. Their skills in a particular field. Ameed nodded and then scrolled down.

2. Acquaintance- is equal to being. - The individual's personal knowledge. Their state of being acquainted. The person or persons with whom one is acquainted.

He thought about that and felt like it was saying the knowledge or skills to communicate with the necessary people should be to ensure success in whatever field the body decides to explore.

3. The Racket- fraudulent scheming enterprises or activities. A slang for occupation or business.

He knew that meant any business that may not be acceptable by normal social standards of government.

4. The Tactical- related to combat tactics, as involving actions or means of less magnitude or at a shorter distance from a base of operations.

Ameed smiled. That would be what Snipes meant about not letting your dirt get thrown back into your face.

5. The Elevation- the height to which something is elevated, as the angular distance of a celestial object above the horizon, in order to be successful.

Ameed knew one had to be projected upwards into the life styles of the wealthy.

6. The Loyalist- one who is or remains loyal to a political cause, party, government or sovereign.

In Ameed's mind, loyalty was unwavering allegiance. Being faithful to a person, a cause, ideal or way of life.

The information on the computer went on to say that there are usually two governing heads to be recognized, calling them the mind and the brain. The mind is the element in an individual that is intelligent, perceives and thinks. It is carful reasoning. While the brain is the portion of the vertebrate's central nervous system that constitutes the organ of thought and coordination. In other words, the brain controls the body.

Ameed processed all of this information. From the way he was looking at it, Snipes would pretty much be like the mind, seeing as he somehow had the type of mind to reason things out and put them into the best and most logical position. Whereas he was more like the brain.

Ameed knew that he was more of a *Corporate Street Thug* than anything else. Which was why he somehow kept one foot in the streets. He wasn't like Snipes, who could politic with the best of the white-collar criminals.

That caused him to smile though, he was thinking about this trip that he was about to make. After the wedding, he was going to South America to meet some people, which was why he was trying to get a better understanding of the Cartel.

Trai'Quan

Chapter Eighteen

The restaurant was located in Stillwater, Oklahoma, area code 405 to those who happen to know. The people inside were completely oblivious to the actual goings on, not that there was a need for one to pay immediate attention to anything, there wasn't. It was indeed natural for four elderly Italians to enter wearing $2000, tailored made, suits and $800 dress shoes. There was nothing at all strange about the waiter showing them to a secluded table near the very back, where the lighting was very dim because it was lit mostly by candle light. It was actually a setting that was meant for a romantic date.

The waiter excused himself once the four men were seated and they waited, not wanting to start their meeting in the presence of the younger man. In fact, they waited five full minutes before the first word was even spoken.

"Alright, Caesar, you called for this meeting, bringing everyone way out here to the middle of nowhere. So, tell us, what's it really about?"

Caesar, being the oldest of the four was the one they looked to whenever there was some type of problem or issues in the air. He was the oldest of those to come from the old country and he had what some referred to as the Royal, pure, Sicilian Blood flowing through his body. His face showed his ancient, with the wrinkles and weather worn skin, but Caesar didn't really move like his age. Instead of moving like a 90-year-old man, he could walk like he was 65.

Caesar looked at each one of them carefully. The tallest of them would be Angelous, who lived in Sacramento, CA. Then there was Mariano, who was nearly Caesar's age, he was short and stocky. Lastly was Frankie, who was not only the youngest one present but also the most dangerous. Frankie lived in Lansing, MI. and Mariano lived in Syracuse, NY.

"I realize that you old men may be very busy these days." Caesar looked into each one of their faces. "But I've come across some very interesting information that you may be curious about." No one spoke, instead they all waited for him to continue.

Seeing as their position here in the states was nearly secret, they weren't Capo's nor Don's, these four men were simply called Elders. Theirs wasn't the same power as the power of a Capo or a Don, the Elders were official representatives for the Sicilian and Corsican Mafia here, in the United States. The decisions they made, *if* they got involved in any of the family's business, would or could be life changing.

"You've all heard about the Peralli family, the murders which were exceptionally carried out. In other words, a professional touch was used there," he said and watched as three old heads nodded. "The Corsican council is concerned with the possible war that could be building between the Italians and the Irish, who we've also learned are in bed with the Russian's."

"You mean that cute tall glass of water? The one with the long legs and expensive taste?" Mariano asked.

"She's a mean Russian bitch, too."

Caesar looked over at him with a funny look on his face.

"How did this thing with the Irish get started in the first place?" Angelous asked.

For a moment, they all watched Caesar, waiting to see what he would say.

Caesar was deep into his own thoughts at the moment. Then he cleared his throat and spoke, "From what Don Sirrelli tells me, Parilli's son was working for the Irish at the warehouses, where they were manufacturing funny money. Some of it came up missing and Donnie, the son, also disappeared. One thing caused another." Caesar held his hands up.

"I heard," Frankie put in. "A good many of the Irish were killed at this warehouse."

At the same time that the four Elders met to discuss the issue, Louis Sirrelli looked up from behind his desk into the face of the Brooklyn Capo, Charlie.

"Listen, Don Sirrelli," Charlie started. "I had no idea that Peralli' brought you into this mess and I wanna apologize to you."

Sirrelli nodded his head but didn't speak. He'd learned of Charlie's involvement in the whole thing when Merrick was investigating things for him and it came as a surprise that Charlie's greed allowed him to use little Donnie the way he had.

"Do you realize that you are the real reason all of these people are dead? On top of all that, your own Don doesn't even know how filthy you are. Had we gone to war, would you have come forward with all of this?"

"Uh, Mr. Sirrelli, I uh," he stuttered

"Exactly," Sirrelli stated. "So, tell me, why do you think I shouldn't have you wacked as a favor to your Don? Seeing as you may one day be the cause of his down fall." He watched as Charlie looked confused, almost as if he didn't know if he would live or die tonight.

Caesar wasn't really sure how to perceive the meeting. He walked through his house in Corpus Christi, Texas and entered the den. He had so many thoughts in his mind. Taking a seat in the recliner, he lifted the Columbian smoking pipe off the coffee table, lit it and sat back to think about the situation some more.

They had also discussed the issue of Milan Giovanni being made an Under Boss. Between that decision and the possible conflict with these Irish guys, something had to be done. Caesar could feel it in his bones, there was a war coming and the last time he felt something so strongly he'd still been in the old country, where a war began between some of the other families. He'd witnessed the downfall of one whom he had some pretty strong ties to. He wasn't able to join in, because of what started the war. It had been declared a blood vendetta, one family violated the other in such a way that it became a deadly feud. One where all of the other families had to stand by and watch. To join in, would have been to choose sides and once the sides were chosen, some of the other families would have then joined in. A balance would have been established and whichever family, good or bad, right or wrong, the one who came out on top, stood the chance of being one of the most powerful families in existence. Thus, certain codes of honor would have been invoked.

Caesar had watched as this family, the one he'd held ties to, was destroyed and wiped out by the other family. The winning family's name had been Sirrelli. Back in those days, Caesar hadn't liked the Sirrelli clan, mostly because in his eyes, they were power hungry. Now a days, it was the Sirrelli's who kept a lot of the business aspects in order and they had connections to all the families. Caesar also thought about the wedding invitations. He still hadn't been able to meet this young man that Sirrelli spoke so highly of.

"They're all dead. So how do we collect our fuckin money now?" Jacob asked.

Bobby sat in his chair and watched as Jacob paced back and forth in the room, the realization having just set in. The Italians had sent a runner to inform them that the people responsible for the disrespect were no longer a problem. But the fact that the stolen money would never be recovered didn't quite sit well with the younger brother.

"Fuck! I say we still push them to give us the money back," Jacob stated.

"We both know that they won't do that," Bobby responded.

The truth was, for the Italians to go to the extent of killing a whole family in order to prevent a war, meant that they'd lost more than what the war would have been about. Trying to get them to repay the money would actually give them the upper hand in the war. Then, it wouldn't just be about a few Italians, it would involve nearly all of them.

Bobby knew that Jacob was only stressing because he didn't want to give the Russians anything. With this planned heist for next month, they expected to walk away with a good deal of money or gold and Jacob didn't see the bigger picture.

* * *

"Those plates led back to the Russian Embassy. Which meant, whoever you saw driving those vehicles were Russian," Agent Simkins explained.

They were both standing in the office at the Cattani. Agent Simkins held a glass of Hennessy Black in his hand, while Merrick held a glass with Cîroc in it. The ten-foot window they stood in front of looked down into the Casino but on the outside it was black marble glass.

"Russian's, huh?" Merrick said.

Agent Simkins looked at the younger man, he didn't really ask a lot of questions about what Merrick had his hands into. He was still plagued by the Miami airport heist because he could damn near swear on his mother's undug grave that Merrick had been the one to do it. But the longer he knew the younger man, the more he realized that proving it would be impossible.

"Look, I don't know what you've got going on with the Russian's, but whatever it is, you need to be very careful. These people live close to our laws, but they have laws of their own," Simkins said.

But Merrick had something else on his mind at the moment. He'd had both Luke and Laura come to New York and look into both the Irish and the Russians. From the report he had received a few days ago, he kind of suspected what they were up to. The only reason he didn't tell Agent Simkins that he already knew these people were Russian was because no matter how much business he did with the guy, he was still and always would be a cop and he would never trust a cop.

"Don't worry about it, old man." Merrick laughed. "I'm not in business with them. Our paths barely crossed, that's all and I wanted to know who they were before I did something stupid."

But even as he listened to the explanation, Agent Simkins knew that it was some bullshit. He just didn't know what color the bull was. "Anyway, look. I appreciate what you did for my sister," he said.

They were both watching as Jackie moved through the casino wearing a $2200 Donna Karen business skirt suit, with $1800 Reed Krokoff platforms on. Walking behind her at a respectful distance were two, 6 foot plus, 250 lbs. body guards that Merrick had hired to go everywhere with her.

"I'm almost reconsidering the deal," Merrick said.

"Yeah, she can be a handful," Simkins laughed.

Handful wasn't the right word for it. Not only was Jackie fine for such a short woman. 5 '1" and about 126 lbs., but she had the attitude of a tyrant. Sort of a female version of Napoleon. Short and forceful when she needed to be but she did take her job seriously. She didn't take shit from anyone.

"Nah, she's really an asset," Merrick replied. "I just wish that I could find another one just like her seeing as right now I have her running both casinos. I'm about to secure one in Las Vegas soon, if nothing goes wrong that is."

Agent Simkins whistled. "Muthafucka, you sho you ain't the illest nigga in all of Nebraska?"

To which Merrick shook his head. "Man, you keep high jacking these movies they gone charge yo ass for royalties. I know Denzel wants his swag back," he laughed.

"But seriously," Agent Simkins stop laughing. "I've got to ask you something. Have you decided where you're going to live after the wedding?"

Merrick thought about it, he wasn't sure if it was a trick question or not and Agent Simkins could have sworn that he saw his eye color change to green. He thought they were grey a second ago.

"I was thinking about the house Anna and Jen have been living in."

"Nah. That's a good family spot but, bruh, you've got too much going on to be letting people know where you rest at," Simkins said. "I'm originally from Chicago and I know how organizations think. You make enemies, they can't get you they go after your family. What I'm saying is, you gone need a secure location for your wife."

Merrick gave his words a lot of thought and it made sense the more he thought about it. "So, what do you have in mind?"

"How about you give that house to your partner. His girl just had a son, right?"

"Yeah, little Saykwon," Merrick said proudly of his God son, who he already had plans for.

"Alright," Simkins continued. "Let him live there. He'll be close enough to keep his eye on the rest of your family but you and your wife. Maybe you should move somewhere that isn't so exposed."

It made sense even more now that he was thinking about it like that. Especially after he'd gone to see that psychiatrist the other day. Merrick knew there would be a strong possibly that his other selves would draw enemies. "So, what did you have in mind?"

"Sheeiit, nigga you rich. You can live anywhere in the world you fuckin' choose. But where ever you decide, it has to be comfortable for your wife and secured for your future children."

Merrick was seeing the logic clearly. With the wedding being in three days that didn't leave him a whole lot of time. He thought that maybe Don Sirrelli could help.

Chapter Nineteen
Elizabeth, New Jersey

Elizabeth, New Jersey, which was in Northeast New Jersey and the seat of Union County, was also considered Mob Country seeing as 75% of it was where a lot of Mafia figures made their homes. Especially those who were retired, or those who weren't active in the organized enterprises. Since Merrick was officially adopted by his distant cousin, Francis Cattani the fourth, who was also a long distant in-law to one of the Elders from Corsica, Mariano Gelluseppe, the 86-year-old Providence representative, it was agreed that the wedding would take place close to his great grandmother, Agatha Cattani. It would have taken place at St. Patrick's cathedral in New York, but instead it took place at his great grandmother's church in New Jersey, out of respect for the older woman.

Earlier that year Merrick had filed papers to have the name Cattani added to his name, out of honor to his family. So, his name stood as Merrick Blacksun Cattani. It was the third Saturday in the month of September and it seemed as if every Italian in New Jersey showed up. Which was pretty much in part, due to the fact that Don Sirrelli was also sponsoring Merrick. With his power alone, important people were coming forward to embrace Merrick. Even those who still questioned his half Corsican blood line, they didn't deny it. In all it was a glorious event, one that would be spoken about for years to come.

"Excuse me."

The conversation stopped. Ameed, Judah, Monk and Juan all looked to Merrick, who in turn looked at the slim youthful Italian that came to interrupt their gathering. At the reception, or rather the after-wedding party which was being held at Don

Sirrelli's manor, the five of them somehow seemed to stick together while all around them there were Italians everywhere. Even though they'd accepted Merrick's claim to the bloodline they were still slow about opening their doors completely. Unlike the women folk, all of them, his great grandmother, mother, mother-in-law, sister, sister-in-law's and his wife, seemed to hold all of the attention. It seemed everyone wanted to meet Anna and they were all bearing gifts, or rather, envelopes with money inside of them.

"What can I do for you, li'l man?" Merrick asked.

"Don Sirrelli asked that you accompany him in the study," the Italian said then looked at Juan. "You and your brother-in-law."

Merrick looked at Juan who only hunched his shoulders. They both downed their drinks and excused themselves. Walking side by side, they followed the kid as he led them to a door, which seemed to be at the back of the extremely large estate. Once they were there, he stopped and stood to the side.

Merrick glanced over at Juan once more then stepped forward, grasping the handle of the door and pulling it open. Stepping inside, they saw that it was a rather large library which held a lot of books as well as some antique furniture. There was a large fire place and a nice sized desk. Also present with in the room were the seven men, standing around with drinks in hand and smoking expensive cigars.

Still enjoying the party with the others, Judah asked, "You think they gone beat him up or something?"

Ameed continued to sip his drink. He looked over at Monk, who, as usual, wasn't talking. "I doubt it."

"Probably some Italian ritual or some shit. Might be why they wanted Juan, too," Judah added.

He accepted the explanation, after all it was the guys wedding. Ameed wasn't even thinking about it, his mind was somewhere else. After the wedding and once Merrick had left on his honeymoon, he was taking the jet to South America. He had to attend his own meeting and from what he knew, these Cartel people didn't play games.

* * *

"Now that everyone's present," Don Sirrelli said after he'd introduced the four Elders, Francis, and Milan, Merrick's cousin and father-in-law. "There are two major issues at hand," he continued. "But neither could be solved without the presence of all four of these men, along with myself and Francis." Don Sirrelli turned first to Milan, "Mr. Giovanni, a petition was made by myself to bestow upon you an official rank or position. This position couldn't have been sanctioned by myself alone. Other than presenting it to the Sicilian or Corsican council of Italy, the only other way to make it official is with the approval of these four men." He waved his hand to indicate the four Elders, who were all seated while Don Sirrelli, Francis, Milan, Juan and Merrick were standing in front of the fire place. "Your application has been reviewed and a complete investigation of you has been made. As it stands on this day of September 2010, Milan Giovanni, you are hereby made Governor, presiding officer, of the northern region of the state of Georgia. The question, Mr. Giovanni is...," Don Sirrelli paused in his speech. "Do you fully accept the weight and responsibility of this position?"

When he fell silent, they all watched as Milan gave careful thought to the address.

"Yes, I do," he nodded.

"Then," Don Sirrelli said. "A declaration will be signed this day and copies will be sent to all of the heads of the families, here and abroad. Welcome, Don Milan Giovanni."

They watched as Milan turned and each of the four Elders stood and embraced him. Merrick stood by with Juan and watched the ceremony as it happened. He hadn't known that he would be present, but he was proud of his father-in-law.

Then Don Sirrelli turned to him, "Merrick Blacksun Cattani, you and I have come a long way since first we met. My respect for you has grown tremendously and where some may question your mixed blood line, I myself have learned not to underestimate the Italian blood that flows through you." He stopped talking for a moment and glanced around. "Unfortunately, you're too young to even be considered for the position of a Don. Being a Don, or a Capo, is much more than poking your chest out and barking orders at others. Despite what those imitation organization's out there may think or do, the authority and position of a Don is also one of respect, wisdom and great integrity, all of which are built through one's own character, over an uncounted amount of years. No one can become a Don by felonious acts.

"However, there is another position that is being offered to you today, which also has to be approved by these gentlemen present here. As you've come to know, the state of New Jersey is pretty much run by Don Fabianti, with the exception of Atlantic City, which I myself run. I've actually been running the entire city by myself as of late. I've only got soldiers, some Lieutenant's and Captain's, those who answer to me directly. I could use a good Under Boss. One that I can depend on. One with good judgement and who knows how to make the right decisions when necessary." Don Sirrelli looked straight into Merrick's eyes. "This is a position that answers to me. You'll actually be considered a part of my family. That is, if you can be sure that you're responsible and able to hold this post."

Merrick looked into the older man's eyes. "Only one condition. Respectfully, Don Sirrelli." He dropped his head in a show of respect.

"Continue," Sirrelli granted.

"I'd take the post, if I can have Monk and Juan here as my Captain and Lieutenant. I won't be able to trust those I don't know, but these two I do trust with my life."

This caused Don Sirrelli to laugh. "Done. Merrick Cattani, on this day of September the year 2010, you are here by granted the full power and authority of Under Boss of Atlantic City, subject to my authority alone. A declaration will be signed this day and copies will be sent to all of the families here and abroad. Welcome, Under Boss Cattani."

Anna couldn't believe the gift her husband had given her. Especially after all of the other gifts she'd received, but she stood upon it anyway, smiling from ear to ear. The Oyster was equally black and white, a Yacht that was 70 ft. in length and a little over 35 ft. of beam. LOA 70 '5" with a Lwl 69 '8". It had a mast height of 90 '15", with two large staterooms and twin 125hp Volvo engines. Merrick told her the Yacht cost a little short of three million and she still couldn't believe that it was hers. It even had her name on it, painted in fancy gold letters.

At the moment, the yacht's Captain was talking with Merrick, teaching him how to navigate the boat, while Anna stood on deck, looking out at the sea. She was now Mrs. Cattani and as Merrick recently explained, with the job he'd been given, they would have to find another house. Most likely one in New Jersey. The house in Georgia was being given to Ameed and while her family would be in Georgia, with her father being a Don now, she would have Juan in New Jersey, because he would be with Merrick. Jen was also moving to New Jersey and attending college there so she would have someone there that she knew. Even Jen couldn't believe that he'd given her a boat.

Anna stood on deck, bouncing and rocking with the motion of the water and thinking about her life. Merrick said that she could go to school, too. He was going to have her finish high school and also attend college, but she'd said that she wanted to start building their family, first. So, they were planning their first child.

Chapter Twenty
Afterward, I Want In

The private jet landed at Kennedy Airport in New York City. As soon as it landed it taxied up the tarmac and then the airport workers guided it into one of the large hangers. Waiting inside the hanger, was an armored truck. Once the jet was situated, its cargo was then off loaded and loaded onto the truck. The shipment was that of gold and had been expected.

As the gold was moved off the jet, another shipment of gold was being loaded onto the jet. One shipment was reddish gold and the other was yellow. The entire process didn't take any more than an hour and fifteen minutes, thus two hours after the plane landed, it had been unloaded and then reloaded, refueled and cleared for takeoff again.

While at the same time the armored truck, which was white and black, with the name of the Federal Reserve Bank of New York City on its side, pulled out of the hanger and made the necessary turns to get on to the Highway. There were three men to guard the shipment, it wasn't as if more were needed. It was supposed to be nearly impossible to penetrate the truck in the first place, let alone to know anything about the shipment. So, neither the driver, nor his partner, or the guard that rode in the back, were expecting anything when they turned off on to the side street. A street that was lined with business warehouses and not much traffic. None of them were expecting it when the 2500 Ram pickup truck pulled in front of the armored truck, blocking its path, while another one blocked it from behind.

"Oh! Shit! We're being hit!" The driver yelled.

A third truck, this one actually a van, pulled up right next to the armored truck on its driver side and while the guards inside pushed clips into their AR15's and M-15's, getting ready for what was about to come, one of them tried the radio and saw that it was being jammed. A fourth truck pulled up to block the armored truck in completely, in a box formation, then the side door of the van slid open. A guy holding what looked like a large super soaker water gun in his hands stepped forward as armed gunmen were now lining the streets around the whole scene.

The man with the large toy aimed it at the side of the truck and squeezed the trigger, shooting out a yellowish cream type foam substance, which lathered the side of the truck until it looked like a cake on its side. The whole time the gunmen in the streets were directing traffic around the truck and out of their way. The foam on the side of the truck seem to freeze and began to turn white. It looked as if it was hardening. By this time, another guy stepped out of the van holding a large construction type sludge hammer. He looked at his watch and appeared to be counting, while inside of the armored truck the guards started to panic.

"What are they doing, Joey? What are they doing?" The guard who was riding in back with the gold asked because he couldn't see anything himself. He needed the two up front to tell him what was going on but as they watched through the side view mirror, they still couldn't believe what they were seeing.

"Better brace yourself, David, I believe their coming in," the driver said.

"They're coming in? What the fuck do you mean their coming in? How the fuck are they going to get in?"

But before Joey could explain it to him the guy lifted the sledge hammer and began striking the side of the truck's wall, which seemed to have become brittle.

* * *

In a black on black Escalade EVO, parked two blocks away, Merrick looked over at Monk in the passenger seat. His eyes caught Juan's in the rear-view mirror as they watched the side of the truck cave in. Then one of the gunmen stepped forward and tossed a grenade inside. There was an explosion and then they started to move the gold from the armored truck to the van.

The whole heist looked extremely professional and took approximately twenty-eight minutes after the side caved in. But just as they were finishing up, Merrick lifted the twin FN Five Seven's, which carried twenty 5.7 -28mm armor piercing rounds each.

He looked at Monk and Juan once more then said. "You gotta know I want in, don't you?"

They watched as both of his eyes turned dark grey.

To Be Continued...
Quiet Money 3
Coming Soon

Submission Guideline

Submit the first three chapters of your completed manuscript to ldpsubmissions@gmail.com, subject line: Your book's title. The manuscript must be in a .doc file and sent as an attachment. Document should be in Times New Roman, double spaced and in size 12 font. Also, provide your synopsis and full contact information. If sending multiple submissions, they must each be in a separate email.

Have a story but no way to send it electronically? You can still submit to LDP/Ca$h Presents. Send in the first three chapters, written or typed, of your completed manuscript to:

LDP: Submissions Dept
Po Box 944
Stockbridge, Ga 30281

DO NOT send original manuscript. Must be a duplicate.

Provide your synopsis and a cover letter containing your full contact information.

Thanks for considering LDP and Ca$h Presents.

BOW DOWN TO MY GANGSTA

By **Ca$h**

TORN BETWEEN TWO

By **Coffee**

THE STREETS STAINED MY SOUL **II**

By **Marcellus Allen**

BLOOD OF A BOSS **VI**

SHADOWS OF THE GAME II

By **Askari**

LOYAL TO THE GAME **IV**

By **T.J. & Jelissa**

A DOPEBOY'S PRAYER **II**

By **Eddie "Wolf" Lee**

IF LOVING YOU IS WRONG… **III**

By **Jelissa**

TRUE SAVAGE **VII**

MIDNIGHT CARTEL III

DOPE BOY MAGIC IV

By **Chris Green**

BLAST FOR ME **III**

A SAVAGE DOPEBOY III

CUTTHROAT MAFIA II

By **Ghost**

A HUSTLER'S DECEIT III

KILL ZONE **II**

BAE BELONGS TO ME III

A DOPE BOY'S QUEEN II

By **Aryanna**

COKE KINGS V

KING OF THE TRAP II

By **T.J. Edwards**

GORILLAZ IN THE BAY V

De'Kari

THE STREETS ARE CALLING II

Duquie Wilson

KINGPIN KILLAZ IV

STREET KINGS III

PAID IN BLOOD III

CARTEL KILLAZ IV

DOPE GODS II

Hood Rich

SINS OF A HUSTLA II

ASAD

TRIGGADALE III

Elijah R. Freeman

KINGZ OF THE GAME V

Playa Ray

SLAUGHTER GANG IV

RUTHLESS HEART IV

By Willie Slaughter

THE HEART OF A SAVAGE III

By Jibril Williams

FUK SHYT II

By Blakk Diamond

FEAR MY GANGSTA 5

THE REALEST KILLAS

By Tranay Adams

TRAP GOD II

By Troublesome

YAYO IV

A SHOOTER'S AMBITION III

By S. Allen

GHOST MOB

Stilloan Robinson

KINGPIN DREAMS III

By Paper Boi Rari

CREAM

By Yolanda Moore

SON OF A DOPE FIEND II

By Renta

FOREVER GANGSTA II

GLOCKS ON SATIN SHEETS II

By Adrian Dulan

LOYALTY AIN'T PROMISED II

By Keith Williams

THE PRICE YOU PAY FOR LOVE II

DOPE GIRL MAGIC III

By Destiny Skai

CONFESSIONS OF A GANGSTA II

By Nicholas Lock

I'M NOTHING WITHOUT HIS LOVE II

By Monet Dragun

CAUGHT UP IN THE LIFE III

By Robert Baptiste

LIFE OF A SAVAGE IV

A GANGSTA'S QUR'AN II

By **Romell Tukes**

QUIET MONEY III

By **Trai'Quan**

THE STREETS MADE ME II

By **Larry D. Wright**

THE ULTIMATE SACRIFICE VI

IF YOU CROSSM ME ONCE II

By **Anthony Fields**

THE LIFE OF A HOOD STAR

By Ca$h & Rashia Wilson

Available Now

RESTRAINING ORDER **I & II**

By **CA$H & Coffee**

LOVE KNOWS NO BOUNDARIES **I II & III**

By **Coffee**

RAISED AS A GOON I, II, III & IV

BRED BY THE SLUMS I, II, III

BLAST FOR ME I & II

ROTTEN TO THE CORE I II III

A BRONX TALE I, II, III

DUFFEL BAG CARTEL I II III IV

HEARTLESS GOON I II III IV

A SAVAGE DOPEBOY I II

HEARTLESS GOON I II III

DRUG LORDS I II III

CUTTHROAT MAFIA

By **Ghost**

LAY IT DOWN **I & II**

LAST OF A DYING BREED

BLOOD STAINS OF A SHOTTA I & II III

By **Jamaica**

LOYAL TO THE GAME I II III

LIFE OF SIN I, II III

By **TJ & Jelissa**

BLOODY COMMAS I & II

SKI MASK CARTEL I II & III

KING OF NEW YORK I II,III IV V

RISE TO POWER I II III

COKE KINGS I II III IV

BORN HEARTLESS I II III IV

KING OF THE TRAP

By **T.J. Edwards**

IF LOVING HIM IS WRONG...I & II

LOVE ME EVEN WHEN IT HURTS I II III

By **Jelissa**

WHEN THE STREETS CLAP BACK I & II III

THE HEART OF A SAVAGE I II

By **Jibril Williams**

A DISTINGUISHED THUG STOLE MY HEART I II & III

LOVE SHOULDN'T HURT I II III IV

RENEGADE BOYS I II III IV

PAID IN KARMA I II III

By **Meesha**

A GANGSTER'S CODE I &, II III

A GANGSTER'S SYN I II III

THE SAVAGE LIFE I II III

CHAINED TO THE STREETS I II III

By J-Blunt

PUSH IT TO THE LIMIT

By **Bre' Hayes**

BLOOD OF A BOSS **I, II, III, IV, V**

SHADOWS OF THE GAME

By **Askari**

THE STREETS BLEED MURDER **I, II & III**

THE HEART OF A GANGSTA I II& III

By **Jerry Jackson**

CUM FOR ME I II III IV V

An **LDP Erotica Collaboration**

BRIDE OF A HUSTLA **I II & II**

THE FETTI GIRLS **I, II& III**

CORRUPTED BY A GANGSTA I, II III, IV

BLINDED BY HIS LOVE

THE PRICE YOU PAY FOR LOVE

DOPE GIRL MAGIC I II

By **Destiny Skai**

WHEN A GOOD GIRL GOES BAD

By **Adrienne**

THE COST OF LOYALTY I II III

By Kweli

A GANGSTER'S REVENGE **I II III & IV**

THE BOSS MAN'S DAUGHTERS I II III IV V

A SAVAGE LOVE **I & II**

BAE BELONGS TO ME I II

A HUSTLER'S DECEIT I, II, III

WHAT BAD BITCHES DO I, II, III

SOUL OF A MONSTER I II III

KILL ZONE

A DOPE BOY'S QUEEN

By **Aryanna**

A KINGPIN'S AMBITON

A KINGPIN'S AMBITION **II**

I MURDER FOR THE DOUGH

By **Ambitious**

TRUE SAVAGE I II III IV V VI

DOPE BOY MAGIC I, II, III

MIDNIGHT CARTEL I II

By **Chris Green**

A DOPEBOY'S PRAYER
By **Eddie "Wolf" Lee**
THE KING CARTEL **I, II & III**
By **Frank Gresham**
THESE NIGGAS AIN'T LOYAL **I, II & III**
By **Nikki Tee**
GANGSTA SHYT **I II &III**
By **CATO**
THE ULTIMATE BETRAYAL
By **Phoenix**
BOSS'N UP **I , II & III**
By **Royal Nicole**
I LOVE YOU TO DEATH
By Destiny J
I RIDE FOR MY HITTA
I STILL RIDE FOR MY HITTA
By **Misty Holt**
LOVE & CHASIN' PAPER
By **Qay Crockett**
TO DIE IN VAIN
SINS OF A HUSTLA
By **ASAD**
BROOKLYN HUSTLAZ
By **Boogsy Morina**
BROOKLYN ON LOCK I & II
By **Sonovia**
GANGSTA CITY

By **Teddy Duke**

A DRUG KING AND HIS DIAMOND I & II III

A DOPEMAN'S RICHES

HER MAN, MINE'S TOO I, II

CASH MONEY HO'S

By **Nicole Goosby**

TRAPHOUSE KING **I II & III**

KINGPIN KILLAZ I II III

STREET KINGS I II

PAID IN BLOOD **I II**

CARTEL KILLAZ I II III

DOPE GODS

By **Hood Rich**

LIPSTICK KILLAH **I, II, III**

CRIME OF PASSION I II & III

By **Mimi**

STEADY MOBBN' **I, II, III**

THE STREETS STAINED MY SOUL

By **Marcellus Allen**

WHO SHOT YA **I, II, III**

SON OF A DOPE FIEND

Renta

GORILLAZ IN THE BAY **I II III IV**

TEARS OF A GANGSTA I II

DE'KARI

TRIGGADALE I II

Elijah R. Freeman

GOD BLESS THE TRAPPERS I, II, III

THESE SCANDALOUS STREETS I, II, III

FEAR MY GANGSTA I, II, III IV

THESE STREETS DON'T LOVE NOBODY I, II

BURY ME A G I, II, III, IV, V

A GANGSTA'S EMPIRE I, II, III, IV

THE DOPEMAN'S BODYGAURD I II

Tranay Adams

THE STREETS ARE CALLING

Duquie Wilson

MARRIED TO A BOSS... I II III

By Destiny Skai & Chris Green

KINGZ OF THE GAME I II III IV

Playa Ray

SLAUGHTER GANG I II III

RUTHLESS HEART I II III

By Willie Slaughter

FUK SHYT

By Blakk Diamond

DON'T F#CK WITH MY HEART I II

By Linnea

ADDICTED TO THE DRAMA I II III

By Jamila

YAYO I II III

A SHOOTER'S AMBITION I II

By S. Allen

TRAP GOD

By Troublesome
FOREVER GANGSTA
GLOCKS ON SATIN SHEETS
By Adrian Dulan
TOE TAGZ I II III
By Ah'Million
KINGPIN DREAMS I II
By Paper Boi Rari
CONFESSIONS OF A GANGSTA
By Nicholas Lock
I'M NOTHING WITHOUT HIS LOVE
By Monet Dragun
CAUGHT UP IN THE LIFE I II
By Robert Baptiste
NEW TO THE GAME I II III
By **Malik D. Rice**
LIFE OF A SAVAGE I II III
A GANGSTA'S QUR'AN
By **Romell Tukes**
LOYALTY AIN'T PROMISED
By Keith Williams
QUIET MONEY I II
By **Trai'Quan**
THE STREETS MADE ME
By **Larry D. Wright**
THE ULTIMATE SACRIFICE I, II, III, IV, V
KHADIFI

IF YOU CROSS ME ONCE
By **Anthony Fields**
THE LIFE OF A HOOD STAR
By Ca$h & Rashia Wilson

<u>BOOKS BY LDP'S CEO, CA$H</u>

<u>TRUST IN NO MAN</u>
<u>TRUST IN NO MAN 2</u>
<u>TRUST IN NO MAN 3</u>
<u>BONDED BY BLOOD</u>
<u>SHORTY GOT A THUG</u>
<u>THUGS CRY</u>
<u>THUGS CRY 2</u>
<u>THUGS CRY 3</u>
<u>TRUST NO BITCH</u>
<u>TRUST NO BITCH 2</u>
<u>TRUST NO BITCH 3</u>
<u>TIL MY CASKET DROPS</u>
<u>RESTRAINING ORDER</u>
<u>RESTRAINING ORDER 2</u>
<u>IN LOVE WITH A CONVICT</u>
<u>LIFE OF A HOOD STAR</u>

<u>Coming Soon</u>
BONDED BY BLOOD 2
BOW DOWN TO MY GANGSTA

Trai'Quan

CPSIA information can be obtained
at www.ICGtesting.com
Printed in the USA
LVHW011926080721
692196LV00012B/1507